ENCHANTING EVE

Halloween Romance

DARCI BALOGH

Knowhere Media LLC Denver CO

Chapter One

A cold wind moaned outside Eve's kitchen window. Falling leaves, gold and orange and crisp, blew across the paint peeled porch steps, making skittering sounds until they tumbled to their final resting place in a growing pile outside her front door.

The old house creaked in the storm, but held firm and strong as it had for over 130 years. The trees that canopied the aged home were brilliant with fall color and though another cold winter was on the horizon, fall was currently in its full glory five days before Halloween.

Eve barely noticed the storm outside. Her kitchen was warm with the sweet smells of baking.

Wearing the large apron that had been her father's, her face and hands were smudged with flour. The apron featured a giant crawdad dressed as a chef. Her father had told her he'd bought the apron when on honeymoon in New Orleans with her mother. Handprints of white flour blotched the red cartoon crawdad where Eve had used the apron instead of a dishtowel during her baking frenzy.

Her straight dark hair was pulled back to stay out of her

face while she cooked, but strands of it had come loose and dangled in her eyes. She held a ceramic mixing bowl in one arm. With her other arm she used a large wooden spoon to stir the second batch of cookie dough vigorously. A platter on the counter held a fresh batch of buttery pumpkin shaped sugar cookies. When they cooled she would cover them with orange frosting and pipe them with jack-o'lantern faces.

Eve was deep in the tradition that she and her father had kept since as long as she could remember. Baking these pumpkin cookies for his 7th grade English class at Halloween had been something Albert St. Claire had done his entire 35-year career as a middle school teacher. Eve was determined that this year her father's tradition would continue, even though he was no longer with them.

A particularly strong gust of wind rattled the window-panes making Eve stop what she was doing and look up. Her two black cats, Sabrina and Hazel, also looked towards the window from where they sat on nearby kitchen stools, lazily watching her bake. Hazel, the small and skittish one, hopped down from her perch and began to rub against Eve's ankles while she worked.

"It's just a rainstorm," Eve said. "Nothing to worry about."

The slim black cat meowed at her, whether to agree or disagree was hard to tell. Sabrina, Hazel's jealous and much larger sister, was never one to be outdone. When she saw Eve reach down and scratch Hazel behind her ears, Sabrina shifted her significant cat frame and dropped to the floor with a thump, casually trotting over to Eve in order to get her own ears scratched.

"You two are keeping me from getting my work done," Eve said, but she didn't really mind. These two cats were her only company since her father had died this past spring. Her mother had passed away when she was very young, so young that Eve had no memories of her that hadn't been told to her by her father.

Eve glanced at the wedding picture of her parents that hung on the wall in the small hallway between the kitchen and the living room. For as long as she could remember that picture and others from the family photo album were her only link to her mother. And now pictures were all she had left of her father, too. Eve's eyes filled with tears and she blinked hard to control them.

"We can't get tears in the cookie batter," she said to the cats. "Cookies aren't for sadness."

That's exactly what she told herself when she decided to carry on her father's tradition and bake their annual Halloween cookies for his class. It had been five months since Albert St. Claire suffered a fatal heart attack in his sleep, and Eve figured it was high time she did something more than work and read and sleep and cry. It wasn't going to be easy, but she knew she needed to do it and that her father would want her to get back to a more normal life.

"You're young, you're beautiful, you should be going out and living a fun young person's life." Eve could almost hear his voice.

She sighed. She wasn't all that young anymore, just turned 30. She knew that her father saw her through rose-colored glasses, because she wasn't what you would call beautiful either.

She was neither tall and willowy nor short and spunky. She was average height, too pale, too thin, with dark hair that insisted on being as unbending as possible. And though her eyes were blue, they weren't the kind of eyes one might consider pretty. They were too round and not blue enough to be memorable. Nothing about her was memorable.

She looked around at the old kitchen with its high ceilings, its ancient cupboards with iron knobs, the giant ceramic sink, and the wooden kitchen table with the small blue vase in the center. If things were totally normal her father would have filled that vase with bright orange marigolds from their flowerbeds. Eve hadn't done that. She also hadn't kept up with the garden after her father's death.

She glanced out the window where she could see the volunteer pumpkin plants that had sprouted up on their own and grown into a wild mess. Since she didn't water them in the heat of the summer they had died out and not produced any of the delightful little sugar pumpkins she and her father had always loved.

Her entire backyard was a jungle of dead brown pumpkin vines. Those tangled twisted vines reflected exactly how she felt on the inside.

A knock on the door startled her out of her melodrama. The sister cats, who acted a lot like dogs in Eve's opinion, trotted quickly to the door to greet their visitor.

"Hello, is anyone in there?" A bright and cheery voice sounded through the door followed by another series of rapid knocks.

Eve recognized the voice without looking, Belinda. She pulled open the door to let her friend inside. Belinda's short, stubby frame tumbled into the foyer with the twirling wind and a few sprinkles of raindrops from the storm.

"Oh my gosh, the wind!" Belinda exclaimed, giggling like always.

Belinda was the opposite of Eve. Small and curvy, with short funky blonde hair, dramatic black frame glasses, bright red lipstick and red nails, always dressing in colors and always ready to laugh.

Eve often thought that people were surprised by their long running friendship, which had been strong since 6th grade. But Eve wasn't surprised. Who wouldn't want to be friends with Belinda? It was more surprising, she supposed, that anyone like Belinda would want to be friends with her.

"I'm having a party!" Belinda announced, wiggling her palms in the air like jazz hands.

"A party?"

Belinda reached down to scoop up the sister cats who were meowing and twisting lovingly around her feet.

"I decided that nobody in this town ever does anything fun and if I want to go to a fabulous Halloween party then I need to throw one myself!" Belinda nuzzled her face into the necks of the purring cats and made kissy sounds as she followed Eve into the kitchen, talking the whole time. "You could help me decorate and we'll play games and we'll invite everyone we know. It won't be for kids though. I want it to be a grown up party with grown up refreshments. You know what I mean?" Belinda took in the messy kitchen. "Did Betty Crocker blow up in here?"

Eve smiled. "No, I'm just making some cookies."

Belinda's eyes fell on the giant sized pumpkin cookies. She placed each cat on a stool and pulled the third stool up to the counter. "Are you making your famous pumpkin cookies?" She sounded delighted.

"Yes," Eve shrugged. "I thought maybe I would take them by my Dad's classroom tomorrow. You know, keep up the tradition."

Belinda gave her a pitiful look. "Oh, Evie, that is so sweet." She reached under her glasses and wiped away tears with her carefully manicured fingers. "Your Dad would be thrilled." She sniffed and reached out to pat her friend's hand.

"I just thought it might be..." Eve paused, not certain how to explain, "Fun...maybe."

Belinda broke into a bright smile. "Of course it will be fun! That's great! You really need to get out more."

"Well, it's a start," Eve answered, flouring the surface of the countertop to roll out the next batch.

"Have you met Mr. Murphy yet?" Belinda asked, swiping a piece of cookie dough and popping it into her mouth.

Mr. Murphy was the English teacher who had replaced her father at the middle school. Eve had heard his name, but had not gone out of her way to meet him. She shook her head 'no' and continued rolling out the dough.

"He's really nice," Belinda reassured her. "And he's pretty young and kinda cute." Her eyes flew open with what Eve knew Belinda thought was a wonderful idea. "Maybe we could invite him to the party!"

Eve made a sour face and shook her head. "I'm not sure about a party." She didn't know if she felt up to that much social interaction.

"Please, Evie!" Belinda begged, giving her friend her cutest pleading face. "I need you to help me decorate and pick out a costume and everything."

Eve kept pushing the rolling pin back and forth, meditating on the idea before committing to anything.

"Besides, Chip is going to be there," Belinda added mischievously.

Eve stopped rolling.

"Chip? Chip Hendricks?"

"Yep," Belinda nodded briskly and reached for another blob of cookie dough. "The gossip is that he may be moving back to town permanently and..." she gave a dramatic pause, "He's still single!" Belinda gobbled up the cookie dough, giving her friend an all-knowing smile as she chewed.

Eve didn't respond, but she couldn't deny the tiny butterflies in her stomach at the mention of his name.

"Come on, Evie," Belinda teased. "You're more excited than that, aren't you? We're talking about Chip."

Eve denied Belinda's question with a quick shake of her

head, causing another piece of her ultra straight hair to drop into her eyes, blocking her view. Since her hands were covered in flour and cookie dough, Eve blew at the wayward lock and flicked her head to get it back into place.

"We're not in high school anymore," she chided Belinda.

Belinda grinned naughtily and snatched another bit of dough. "And that is exactly my point."

Eve decided to ignore the teasing. She and Belinda had spent countless hours of their lives giggling over boys. She had other things to do now.

She carefully used the cookie cutter to cut out each pumpkin cookie and placed them on the waiting baking sheet while she listened to Belinda chatter about the Halloween party. Parties weren't really Eve's thing, but as she slid the cookie sheet into the waiting oven she thought maybe Belinda was right, maybe they should throw a Halloween party, maybe it would help her get back to normal.

As if to underscore her decision, a sudden gust of wind blew open the front door and sent a swirl of gold and red fall leaves tumbling into the house.

Chapter Two

The wide sidewalk in front of the school was covered with damp remains from the previous night's storm. Eve followed the familiar path, stepping carefully over multicolored leaves that were scattered across the cement and sodden from the rain.

She wore thick black leggings, a dark orange button up shirt that hung down past her hips, her favorite black leather knee-high boots and a red fall jacket. In her arms she carried a shallow box, and out of the top of that box stuck 30 carefully wrapped giant orange pumpkin cookies with jack o'lantern faces. Belinda had helped her slide each individual cookie into a clear cellophane bag when it was completely decorated. Then they had tied the tops closed with bits of orange yarn from Eve's craft box.

As she approached the school, Eve's heart began to pound in her chest. She had not stepped foot into the middle school where her father had taught her entire life since his death. The principal and teachers, along with his students, had held a memorial for him at the end of the school year, but that had been only weeks after the tragic event and Eve had been too grief-stricken to leave her house at the time. She had sent her regrets and everybody understood. They had all been so very kind.

Eve took a deep breath to try and calm her nerves. This was a happy day. This was the beginning of Halloween celebrations for the children that her father adored teaching.

He was a popular teacher who loved literature and learning and fun. She had enjoyed popping by and surprising him during the day, always catching him in a lively conversation with a student or reading with his great booming voice to his class. Or laughing. Her father had laughed a lot.

Eve took another breath and pushed back the grief. Today was about having fun.

She opened the heavy door at the front of the school and was immediately met with the sights and smells that she remembered so well, not only from her father's tenure there, but from her own years spent as a student in these halls. Mrs. Runyon, the school secretary, spotted her through the large glass window of the front office that looked over the entrance to the school.

"Eve!" Mrs. Runyon exclaimed with pleasure after pushing the sliding glass window open.

"Hi," Eve managed a smile and stepped to the window.

"How are you, dear?" Mrs. Runyon was in her 50's and had worked at the school for over 20 years. Not as long as Eve's father, but long enough that she had been there when Eve was in middle school.

"Fine, thank you," Eve answered. She held up the box of cookies for Mrs. Runyon to see. "I thought I would bring something to Dad's, um, my father's class...for fun," she added.

Through a flutter of 'how nice' and 'isn't that sweet' comments, Mrs. Runyon gave her the front desk's blessing and a special Visitor name tag so she could deliver her goodies to the English class.

Within a few minutes she was standing at the closed door of Room 212-B. Her heart was in her throat, the palms of her hands broke out in a sweat and she felt clammy all over.

Should she knock? She had always walked straight into this room, unannounced and perfectly welcome. This was ridiculous. No reason to be so uncertain. They were just middle school kids and she only wanted to give them some cookies.

The low murmur of a man's voice filtered through the door. Eve raised her hand, made a fist and rapped lightly three times. The low murmur stopped and a few moments later the heavy door swung open with a click and a tug.

"Yes?" A tall man with a shock of dark red hair on his head and a short beard in a slightly lighter shade of red stood in the doorway, looking at her quizzically. He wore a loose crewneck sweater in hunter green, and Eve could see a pale orange shirt collar peeking out from underneath. Green and orange, festive colors for Halloween week.

She stood frozen, unable to form words and feeling like an utter fool. Her hands were so sweaty she worried the box of cookies might slip through them and fall to the floor.

Mutely, she lifted the box and offered the man she assumed was the new teacher, Mr. Murphy, the pumpkin cookies. He glanced at the cookies and back at her, his piercing blue eyes showing a glimmer of humor.

"Are those for me?" he asked.

"I, um, they're pumpkin cookies," Eve said, trying not to stammer. "For the class." She gave him a feeble smile.

Mr. Murphy's face opened with delight. He stepped back while pulling the door wider so Eve could enter and swept his arm up and out in a dramatic gesture. "Welcome, kind Miss!"

Eve heard several giggles from the children at their desks.

She stepped into the classroom and walked to the teacher's desk at the front.

Feeling like she was moving in slow motion, Eve took in the details of what used to be familiar surroundings. The rows of student desks, the laminated posters on the walls, the blackboard with various sentences and book titles scrawled in chalk, the whiteboard in the corner where it appeared children had been drawing pictures of cartoon birds.

The room smelled like she remembered, looked basically like she remembered, but was utterly and completely different.

Placing the box of cookies on the teacher's desk, Eve could see that all of her father's things were gone and had been replaced by what must be Mr. Murphy's books, paperwork and teacher knick knacks. Of course, this is what should be expected. But somehow seeing it made Eve feel like she had swallowed a bag of rocks.

"I'm Mr. Murphy," Mr. Murphy offered. He stuck out his hand to shake hers and Eve discreetly rubbed her palm on her jacket as she reached to take his, afraid that her handshake would be wet and cold.

"I'm Eve St. Claire," Eve said. There was no reaction on Mr. Murphy's part and she realized that he must not know her name. He took her hand however, and gave it a warm shake.

"Well thank you for the cookies. They look delicious."

"That's Mr. St. Claire's daughter," one of the girls, Ruby, whom Eve recognized as a regular customer at the bookstore where she worked, whispered loudly to Mr. Murphy. His eyebrows shot up as he got the hint. He was still holding Eve's hand and he looked at her with both interest and concern.

"Albert St. Claire's daughter?" he asked.

Eve nodded.

There was an awkward pause while Eve returned Mr. Murphy's rather intimate stare with what she hoped was a serene and dignified countenance. As she looked at him, she noticed that he was young, well, younger than most of the other teachers at the school.

His face was moderately handsome, his eyes a kind blue, and his build under that loose green sweater seemed trim and masculine. In general, he looked like an educated, slightly rumpled, teacherly type of person. His red hair and beard were definitely his most dramatic features. Her hand grew warm in his.

"I'm sorry." He let go of her hand and stepped around her to pull out the chair at the desk. "Please, have a seat. It's very nice of you to come by."

"Thank you." She sat down and looked towards the children in their seats. A few of them were watching her and Mr. Murphy, most of them were eyeing the cookies.

"My father and I always made pumpkin cookies for his class at Halloween," Eve felt the need to explain her presence.

"How kind of you." Mr. Murphy turned towards the box of cookies. He pulled one of the festive cellophane bags out of the box to inspect it. "These look delicious," he said as he smiled at her. "Thank you."

"You're welcome," she responded. She smiled briefly at the kids, who were now all watching Mr. Murphy, and thought she should probably make her exit. She moved to stand up.

"Don't go," Mr. Murphy requested. "Please, join us. Ruby, Michael, would you please hand out these cookies to everyone? One per person." Mr. Murphy grabbed another bag out of the box before moving a royal blue plastic chair that sat at the side of his desk into a position so he could sit next to Eve and look out over the classroom. He handed her one of the cookies. "Would you like a cup of coffee to go with that?"

Soon Eve was sitting at her father's old desk, in her father's old chair with a steaming hot styrofoam cup of coffee and a bright orange pumpkin cookie in front of her. The familiarity of the whole experience was a little overwhelming, but also comforting. There were 24 children all milling around the room, chatting happily with each other and enjoying their homemade Halloween treat. Her father would have loved the scene and that thought made her smile.

Mr. Murphy ate the first half of his cookie in two big bites. He munched quietly next to her while watching over the children. He swallowed a sip of coffee from a stainless steel travel mug.

"We were just getting started reading some Poe," he said. "Would you like to stay for that?"

Eve loved Edgar Allan Poe. It was an old family favorite at this time of year.

"Which one are you reading? The Raven? The Tell-Tale Heart?"

"The Raven, today," Mr. Murphy answered.

Eve's gaze swept over the children, who all looked quite young and innocent. She tried to remember when she first read Edgar Allen Poe.

"That's not too dark for them?" she asked.

Mr. Murphy looked at her with mild surprise. "Well, it is the season of Halloween." He cocked his head at her in a teasing manner. "This coming from a woman who lives in a haunted house?" He smiled then popped another large chunk of cookie into his mouth.

Now it was Eve's turn to be surprised. What did he mean by that? How did Mr. Murphy know where she lived, and why would he think that her beautiful old house was haunted?

"Why do you say that?"

"Isn't your house the famous haunted house?" Mr. Murphy responded, perplexed. He looked out at his class as if for verification, but they weren't paying much attention. "Sorry," he offered when he took in her discomfort. "I didn't mean to offend you." He gestured towards the children. "They told me that Mr. St. Claire and his daughter lived in the big old house at the end of Pennsylvania and that the house was haunted."

Eve sat up straighter, as if being proper would somehow diffuse this rumor. She lifted the styrofoam cup in her hands and shook her head slightly, "It's a very old, very beautiful house, but it's definitely not haunted." She took a defiant sip of her coffee.

Ruby, who had been eavesdropping on their conversation, piped up, "Mr. St. Claire told us it was haunted."

Stunned into silence, Eve stared at the little girl. A few of the girl's little friends nodded earnestly in agreement and a number of the other children spoke up at the same time.

"He always told us about it at Halloween."

"My big brother said he told them he lived in a haunted house when he took this class."

"Your house is famous."

"Your house is haunted!"

Eve felt a burning in her cheeks and she wondered why her father would tell these children, why he would tell anyone, that kind of thing. Had he been telling haunted stories about their beloved house as long as he was a teacher?

Mr. Murphy watched her carefully and when he realized she was flustered by the children's comments, he stood up and grabbed a worn book off of the desk.

"All right let's get back to work," he declared. The children made their way back to their desks, some still carrying their treat, some already done eating. "I'll read while you finish eating." Mr. Murphy gave Eve a quick smile as he instructed the class.

Eve stayed for the reading. It seemed rude to leave. She

watched as Mr. Murphy read Poe's 'The Raven' with a commanding tone and complete with a squawking raven's voice, but she wasn't really listening.

She nibbled at her pumpkin cookie and sipped her coffee, but the whole time she was wondering why her father had told those stories to the children of their town. Did the whole town think that her house was haunted? Had he meant it as a joke or had he actually believed it was true? The whole situation bothered her, but the thing that bothered her most was that she had never known. Her own father had never told her anything about them living in a haunted house.

Chapter Three

There was something comforting about a stack of old books. The stack currently in front of Eve included all different types of fiction; romance, fantasy, sci-fi, children's books. It also included some non-fiction; health books, business books, books on how to lose weight and some on how to find love. The stack of books was precariously balanced on a wheeled cart, which Eve pushed carefully through the narrow aisles of the bookstore. When she found the section that a book belonged in, she took it from the cart and added it to the shelf.

This was the only used bookstore in their town. It was the only bookstore of any kind in their town, in fact. Eve had worked here since high school. First as a part-time cashier, then after she returned from college she had taken over as manager.

As jobs went it was perfectly suited for Eve's personality and interests. As a career it was mostly dead end, but then so were almost all of the jobs in their town. For a young woman with an English Lit degree, who was not interested in being a teacher, it was about as spot on a job as she could expect.

The bookstore bought used books for pennies and turned around to sell them, either in person or online, for a few dollars. They also assisted the older generation in town with navigating online purchases of both new and used books. But their biggest draws were the comfortable chairs and sofas placed around the store and the sale of fresh coffee, tea, scones and cookies. They played classical or jazz or sometimes French bistro music, and patrons could sit and read as long as they desired. Eve loved spending time in the bookstore.

Today she was a bit preoccupied with thoughts of her father and his haunted house stories. As she made her way through each aisle, she wondered if the entire town thought her house was haunted and, if so, what exactly did they think of her? She was a single woman, admittedly introverted, a little dark in her sense of humor who loved Halloween and owned two black cats, cats that happened to be named after famous witch characters. She shook her head at the ridiculous idea that she was some kind of haunted character in a fictional story, but she had to admit, from the outside looking in, it was possible people thought of her that way.

Eve glanced at the overstuffed denim blue chair in the corner where one of their regulars, Joanna, a retired post office employee was quietly reading. Joanna spent at least three days a week munching scones and sipping tea while reading romance novels and books on exotic travel, and Eve knew she wouldn't mind an interruption. Eve pushed her cart in Joanna's direction and when the woman looked up and acknowledged her with a friendly nod, Eve sat down in the dark red chair next to hers.

"Have you ever heard the rumor that my house is haunted?" Eve asked.

Joanna let her open book rest in her lap and looked over the top of her bejeweled reading glasses at Eve.

"Yes," she said matter-of-factly. "Everyone knows that."

"What? How can everyone know that? It's not even true!"

Joanna thought for a few moments before answering, "Your Dad used to talk about it all the time. That must be where the rumors started." She gave Eve a kind smile. "You know how he liked to tell stories."

Eve opened her mouth to protest the validity of the haunting rumor, but was interrupted by the sound of bells. A small bundle of bells hung from the front door of the store and jingled when it opened. From where she sat she couldn't see who had come in, so she stood up and went to the front counter leaving Joanna to go back to her reading.

At first glance, Eve only saw a tall, dark businessman standing in the front, looking around at the store. When he turned to face her, however, she realized with more than a little surprise that the businessman was Chip Hendricks. Chip, captain of their high school football team, president of their senior class, son of one of the richest men in town, general heartthrob and Eve's school girl crush, was standing at the counter.

"Chip!" Eve was so surprised she almost shouted his name. Out of the corner of her eye, she saw Joanna leaning forward to peer at the commotion. Eve blushed slightly at her outburst. Chip smiled in a half grin, half smirk kind of way. She lowered her voice, "What are you doing here?"

"I'm back home for an extended visit. Thought I'd stop by and see if you're still here," he said. His voice was soft and smoky and sent nervous flutters through her stomach.

"Yeah," she shrugged lightly and looked around the bookstore, which suddenly seemed a little dusty and dumpy. "Still here."

Chip let his eyes wander down her body, taking her in. She felt unusually exposed under his gaze even though she wore a modest T-shirt style dress that didn't show much of her figure, not that she had much of a figure to show. Eve glanced around shyly to see if anybody was watching. Joanna was back to reading. There were only a half dozen more patrons in the store and all of them had their noses in a book. When she looked back, Chip was giving her that same smirky grin.

"You look good," he said.

She felt heat rise in her cheeks and hated the fact that she was about to appear silly and juvenile by blushing in front of him. She didn't want him to know she was flustered, so Eve took a moment to let her eyes boldly wander up and down his body. She noticed his very nice dark grey suit that was well cut to his tall, wide shouldered form. She took in his black and silver tie, his neatly trimmed, thick, dark hair, his deep brown eyes and closely shaven face that perfectly showed off his square jaw and nicely formed lips. She had to concentrate to keep from sighing.

"You too." She tried to use a confident, sensual tone. She was no longer in high school, after all.

"Catching up on your reading?" Chip nodded his head towards the book she held in her hand.

Eve looked down. It was one of the self-help books she'd been putting away and forgotten she was holding. The title was encased in a giant, bubble heart and read, 'How to Find Love in 30 Days". Eve hurriedly set it on the shelf behind the counter out of sight and ignored the teasing look in Chip's eyes. She cleared her throat and tried to think of something to say. Nothing came to her. He caught her eye and held it with a deep, smoldering gaze. They looked at each other for a long moment. Just when she thought she might start batting her eyelashes uncontrollably at him, the front door banged open, bells jingling madly.

"Chip!" Belinda exclaimed, drawing the attention of all seven book lovers in the store.

Chip lifted his eyebrows and turned to see who was

calling his name. Belinda practically danced to the front counter, her blonde hair was pulled up in an orange bandana that had small jack-o-lanterns in place of polka dots, and she wore a tight grey T-shirt that had sequins in the form of a black cat on the front. She opened her arms wide and went in for the hug. Chip had no choice but to hug her back.

"Belinda," he said, pushing her out to arms length, his calm, cool demeanor barely dented by her bubbly greeting.

"It's so good to see you!" Belinda said, still loud, still attracting everyone's attention.

Now that Belinda was safely removed from him, Chip leaned against the counter, giving Eve an amused glance. Belinda reached up and stroked the sleeve of his suit jacket.

"What are you all dressed up for on a weekday?" She cooed.

Chip straightened his tie with mock importance. "A little board meeting at the old man's company."

The Hendricks family owned a grocery store, two gas stations and a liquor store in town. Chip, it was said, had moved to Chicago after college and worked his way up the ladder at an insurance and investment company. Not too bad for the hometown heartthrob.

"Well, it's very nice. Nice enough to wear to my Halloween party and be Bruce Wayne," Belinda suggested. "You're invited." She reached into her shining patent leather purse and pulled out an index card sized invitation, handing it to him. "Or you could come as Batman!"

Chip grinned, skimming the information on the invitation. He gave Eve a meaningful look. "Are you going?"

"Of course she's going," Belinda answered.

Again, his eyes slid down the front of Eve's chest, making her pulse quicken.

"What are you wearing to the party?" He asked.

"Um..." Eve's mind had gone blank.

"It's a surprise," Belinda saved her. "You'll have to come to the party to find out."

Chip assured them that he would be at the Halloween party before leaving. As soon as he walked out the door and past the giant window at the front of the bookstore, Belinda started tiny hopping up and down with excitement.

"Now you have to come," Belinda commanded.

Eve knew she was right. Though parties weren't her strong point, the draw of Chip being there was enough for Eve to want to at least make the effort to show up.

"I don't have any idea what to wear for a costume," Eve said.

"Don't worry about that," Belinda said confidently. "I know exactly what you should wear."

Chapter Four

Dusk was falling and the lamppost in front of Eve's house was already glowing, fending off the coming night. As dark came sooner this time of year, she had taken to leaving a light on in the living room. She walked carefully across the uneven cobblestones that led up to her front door, taking in the overgrown vegetation in her front yard that had already died back for the year and turned various shades of brown.

The wild pumpkin plants from her backyard had stretched their grasping vines around the house to the front. They combined with the rose bushes she had not pruned, the ivy that had spread across the ground and up one side of the house, and other various weeds and grasses she had neglected to mow this past summer. The result was a tangled mess where there used to be a mature and stately front lawn.

The house was a Victorian built with stone. It had a swirling iron fence, high peaked roof, tall windows and a balcony over the front door where you could walk out from her bedroom upstairs and look down at the street below.

Ancient oak and maple trees loomed on either side of the house. Their leaves had turned to crimson and gold and begun dropping, leaving wispy piles all over the ground. The moon, which would reach full status in a few nights, Halloween to be exact, rose behind the roof, half hidden by the pointed peaks and narrow brick chimneys.

As she got closer she could see Hazel and Sabrina, black and beautiful, watching for her as they sat in the living room window. They were silhouetted by the lamplight that spilled out of the window and their eyes shone yellow. Eve had to admit the whole effect did look very much like your classic haunted house. She chuckled a little at the idea of her father, tall and boisterous, weaving tales of strange sounds and ghost sightings and thrilling his students with scary stories.

Eve had always had a vivid imagination. Encouraged by her father to read, she loved stories and books and movies of all kinds. She had always liked living in a house with such character. They had both loved living in this house, but Eve also had a logical streak and, imagination or not, she certainly didn't believe in ghosts.

In the kitchen, she placed the copper tea kettle on the stove and turned on the gas flame underneath. She started to reach for a mug and a single tea bag, but decided instead to make a whole pot. It had been a chilly day and was getting even chillier outside. Eve pulled down the olive green teapot that had once been her mother's, and filled the bottom with pumpkin spice herbal tea. Why not, she thought to herself, it is almost Halloween after all.

"The wind is picking up outside," she said to the cats, who were winding themselves around her ankles. "Are you hungry?"

She opened the cupboard that held their canned cat food and they both started meowing in excitement, Sabrina most of all. After filling both of their dishes, Eve fixed herself a few slices of bread with cheese on top that she popped into the oven to toast. Steam poured out of the tea kettle as a gust of wind rattled the kitchen window. Darkness had fallen. Eve gazed out of her kitchen window at the moonlit backyard, waiting for the kettle to get to full boil and thinking about Chip Hendricks.

Seeing him today, the way he talked to her, the way he looked at her, had left her in a bit of a shambles. Her stomach felt tight and there was a pleasant lightheadedness she experienced whenever she relived the moments he had smiled at her or the sound of his voice.

Eve had suffered with a mad crush on Chip ever since they were in elementary school together. He had been dark and moody then, and only grown into a darker, moodier, extremely sexy man. Nothing had ever happened between them. In fact, Eve had always thought he either didn't notice her much or thought of her like he would an ugly duckling cousin. Her heart had never given up its romantic dream of him, and even though it had been a few years since she'd seen him, she wondered if maybe this time was the time they would finally end up together. As much as she loved her home and her job and her town, Chip Hendricks was the kind of man that could make a woman seriously consider changing her whole life.

A strong gust of wind hit her house at the exact same moment the boiling kettle started to scream and a loud knocking came at her front door. Eve jumped at the sounds, as did Hazel and Sabrina. Instead of darting off and hiding under the couch as cats normally did when frightened, Hazel and Sabrina ran to the front door meowing loudly. The knocking came again. Eve turned off the gas under the kettle and went to the door, a tiny piece of her wondering if she'd somehow conjured up Chip Hendricks on her front porch.

That particular hope was squelched as soon and she saw

the shock of red hair through the small window at the top of the great wooden front door. She looked more closely through the beveled glass and could make out a semi-familiar face. It took her a few moments, then it hit her, Mr. Murphy was waiting patiently in the wind. She opened the door.

"Mr. Murphy?"

"Hello!" He exclaimed. He was dressed in a casual dark brown leather jacket that looked more like daywear than anything that would keep a person warm. He had no gloves, scarf or hat. This late October wind held a frost in it and had turned his uncovered ears bright red. "Sorry for the intrusion, Miss St. Claire."

"Come out of the wind," Eve answered, stepping back and ushering him into the foyer.

"It gets cold once the sun goes down, doesn't it?" He said as he gratefully stepped inside. He rubbed his hands together, cupped them and blew into them, trying to warm up. He was quite windblown and all the tips of him were burning a bright red from the cold. He reminded Eve of an elf. A tall, well-built elf. His blue eyes twinkled as he smiled at her then looked down at Hazel and Sabrina who were madly twisting their furry bodies around his boots and pulling at the bottom of his jeans with their claws. "And who are these lovely beast-ies?" He asked. As if to introduce herself, Hazel leapt from the floor to his chest where he caught her deftly.

Eve looked at him with surprise. "She's never done that before. Hazel, come here." Eve reached for her.

"I don't mind," Mr. Murphy said, smiling at the purring feline in his arms and the plumper Sabrina who still curled around his feet, meowing loudly because she was unable to make the leap up like her sister. "Cats have a thing for me. Probably because I have a thing for them."

Taking in his chilled exterior, Eve thought it best to invite him to have some tea. She poured water from the kettle into her mother's teapot as Mr. Murphy settled himself at the kitchen table. He happily entertained both cats, who continued to beg for his attention, as he took in the large cozy kitchen with its copper pots and braided rugs and the great white gas stove where Eve prepared the tea.

"You have a beautiful house," he told her as she placed a tray holding the teapot, two cups, cream, sugar and two spoons on the table in front of him.

"Thank you," she smiled, then remembered the rumors. "Do you think it seems haunted now that you've seen it?" Eve meant it as a joke, kind of, but realized too late that she may sound overly sensitive.

He gave her an embarrassed smile. "Sorry, again, for that. I took it as a sort of fun, small town legend. I thought you knew about it. I don't go in for gossip."

Now she was embarrassed. It was hardly Mr. Murphy's fault. He'd just moved into town a few short months ago.

"Actually," he said as he took another look around the kitchen, "I think it's enchanting."

She shrugged nonchalantly, wanting to move on to another subject.

"How can I help you this evening, Mr. Murphy?"

"Please call me Atticus."

"Atticus?" A literary name.

Bashful, he took the cup she offered him and didn't look up. "Yes, Atticus," he gave a wistful sigh. "My mother wanted me to be brilliant."

Eve smiled and poured some tea into his cup, then her own.

"Call me Eve," she said. Then she tried again, "How can I help you tonight...Atticus?"

Happy to be off the subject of his name, Atticus sat back a bit in his chair to look at her. His jacket hung by the front door and he sported a robin's egg blue dress shirt, rolled up at the sleeves. The blue brought out his eyes and she liked how he wore his clothes, casual and a little dressed up all at the same time.

"I was wondering...well, the class and I were wondering...if you would like to come with us to the pumpkin patch day after tomorrow," he raised his brow with the question, "to pick pumpkins?"

Eve was stirring sugar into her tea, enjoying this chat with Atticus at her cozy kitchen table as the cold night enveloped the house. She was flattered at the invitation. Every year, for so many years, she had accompanied her father and his class on their traditional pumpkin picking field trip. She had assumed all of those traditions were gone forever. She started to answer, but was overcome by nostalgia. Big tears welled up in her eyes and she couldn't meet Atticus' gaze.

"I'm sorry," she whispered, fumbling for a napkin. Atticus pulled one from the holder on the table and placed it in her hand.

"Don't be sorry," he said softly. "I didn't mean to upset you. I thought...we thought...it might be fun." He gave her a crooked, hopeful look that made her smile through her tears.

"It does sound fun," she agreed, wiping her eyes and sniffing.

"So, you'll come?" Atticus looked genuinely delighted and Eve nodded at him as she blew her nose on the napkin. Atticus' expression changed suddenly to concern as he sniffed the air, "Do I smell smoke?"

"Cheese toast!" She exclaimed, and jumped up from the table.

Smoke poured from the oven when she opened the door. Atticus waved the smoke away with a dishtowel while Eve popped on an oven mitt and pulled the cookie sheet full of bubbling, blackened cheese out of the oven. She carried the smoking mess to the back porch while Atticus opened the windows from inside the kitchen. They both did their best to fan the smoke out of the windows, but the cold, fall wind did most of the work as it swept through the room.

After the excitement was over and the kitchen was back to normal, Eve fed the two pieces of cooled burned toast that had been her dinner to the cats and fixed four new pieces. Two for her and two for Atticus.

"Toasted cheese is delicious," Atticus declared. "It reminds me of Heidi."

"Me too!" Eve replied, "I made my Dad learn how to make it after he read me Heidi when I was little."

"Are these your parents?" Atticus stood with a fresh cup of tea in his hand looking at her parent's wedding picture on the wall.

"Yes." She set the egg timer to four minutes and joined him in the tiny hallway where the picture hung. He seemed taller, maybe because they were standing in such a small space together. She looked at the image of her mother, so small and delicate, with wide, pale eyes looking so lovingly up at her young father. His strong features, dark hair that tended to curl into a wild frizzy mess, and huge beaming smile that took over the room had already been part of his giant personality, even when they were so young.

"I've heard a lot about your father," Atticus said. "The kids tell me all kinds of stories about him."

She nodded, feeling the tears coming again. She didn't want to cry a second time in front of Atticus, so she chose not to talk at all. She just smiled and nodded.

"He was a great teacher," Atticus continued.

Eve swallowed hard and managed to answer, her voice faltering the tiniest bit, "Yes, he was. He really loved teaching." That was all she could manage to say without collapsing into a weeping mess. When she finally composed herself and glanced at Atticus he was still looking at the picture, seeming to understand the intimacy of the moment. He sensed her gaze and turned towards her, the gentle kindness in his eyes made her feel warm.

"You were lucky to have each other," he said, and he was right.

Chapter Five

"But won't my skin have to be green?" Eve asked as she stood in front of the full-length mirror.

"Technically, yes," Belinda answered.

"I don't know that I want to paint myself green." Eve screwed up her face at the idea as she looked at her reflection. She wore a long sleeved, mid-calf, tight fitting black dress, which Belinda had picked out as the basis of her Halloween costume. Belinda stood next to her wearing a white glittering cocktail dress that poofed out at her waist like a 1950's prom dress. She had found both of these gems at the thrift store and was presenting Eve with her Halloween costume concept.

Belinda wanted them to have partner costumes for her party, which wasn't a totally abhorrent idea to Eve. They were to be Glinda and Elphie, from the popular musical, Wicked. Eve would be Elphie, the green skinned wicked witch in the making with a long, black dress. Belinda would be the good witch, Glinda, with a white dress, tiara and magic wand.

Belinda was a talented seamstress, who made many of her most over the top and fashionably outlandish outfits either from scratch or from altering existing pieces. There was no question Belinda could make the appropriate alterations to these thrift store dresses and turn them into the desired witch outfits. Eve just wasn't sure she wanted to paint herself green as part of the bargain.

"We'll do it in a pretty way," Belinda explained. "I'll have to wear some glitter makeup to be Glinda. We'll just tint some of it green and you can use that."

Eve looked at her friend with some uncertainty. Was one shade of green really better than another?

"Don't worry," Belinda reassured her. "I know you want to look smashing for Chip." Belinda looked at her own stocky, abundantly curvy figure in the white cocktail dress and smoothed her hand over the material. "We all do."

"We all do? That's kind of pathetic, don't you think?" Eve asked.

"It's not pathetic," Belinda answered. "He's the biggest thing to visit this town in months! It gives us all something to shoot for, even though everyone knows you're the one with the best chance of hooking him."

Eve's stomach twisted in an excited knot at Belinda's comment, then she shook her head in denial. "I don't think that's true. Besides, is hooking a man something we should be worrying about as modern, intelligent women?"

"Hooking that man is any woman's dream, no matter how modern and intelligent she is," Belinda declared. "He's tall, dark, handsome, rich, I mean what else can you ask for?"

Funny. Kind. Well-read. Intelligent. A whole slew of attributes flooded through Eve's mind, but she didn't say them out loud. Tall, dark and handsome weren't anything to sneeze at and she had to admit that the idea of hooking Chip gave her serious butterflies.

"So, are you good with your costume?" Belinda asked.

Eve sighed and took another look at their reflection. She looked meek and pale in the black dress, especially next to Belinda with her bouncing white gown and the bright makeup she always wore. Still, the black dress did fit her well and it was better than dressing up as a clown or a French maid.

"Yes, seeing as you already bought it and I have no clue what else to wear, this will be just fine," Eve said.

"Great! I'll take it home and fix it up. You can try it on again before the party to make sure it works. And I have a hat you can use!"

Perfect. A witch's hat and green glitter makeup. Eve wasn't sure if her Halloween costume would be what you'd call man magnet material.

As they shopped at the local Walgreens for party decorations, Belinda chatted happily about all of the RSVPs flooding in for her party. She picked up a fake, plastic pumpkin with an electric, blinking light inside and showed it to Eve.

"What do you think?"

Eve wrinkled her nose. "Why don't you use real pumpkins?"

"I don't have enough time to carve a bunch of real pumpkins. Besides, they're not as bright." Belinda tossed five of the plastic, blinking pumpkins into her shopping cart. "Do you have pumpkins this year? You could bring them to the party...maybe we could have a pumpkin carving contest!" Belinda became instantly jazzed at her idea.

Eve shook her head, "No. I kind of failed at the garden this year. Some volunteer pumpkin plants grew, but I didn't take care of them." Belinda looked disappointed at Eve's confession. "I am going to that pumpkin patch south of town with the school tomorrow. I could pick some up for you," Eve offered.

"You're going to the pumpkin patch with the school?" Belinda asked.

Eve felt her cheeks get hot. She knew Mr. Mur–Atticus had only asked her to come along to be nice, because he knew about her taking part in the school traditions with her father for so long. But she had a feeling Belinda would read something into his invitation, like it was a budding romance.

"Yeah," Eve shrugged nonchalantly. "They asked if I wanted to come on their field trip, since I've gone with them for so many years." Belinda seemed to accept this explanation. Either that or she was distracted by the several options of Halloween garland she was inspecting; black cats, ghosts or witch hats. "That reminds me," Eve recalled, "Did you know that my Dad told everyone our house was haunted?"

Belinda looked at her with some curiosity. "Yes, you didn't?"

"No!" Eve was half amused and half frustrated. "Since when?"

"Since...always, really," Belinda responded, searching her mind for the answer. "I've always known your house as the haunted house."

"You can't be serious," Eve flat out denied her friend's statement.

"Everyone knows it's the haunted house," Belinda continued. Suddenly, her eyes flew open. "It would be a great place for a Halloween party!" She reached out and squeezed Eve's arm as she jumped tiny jumps up and down in glee.

"No," Eve answered automatically, shaking her head to emphasize the point. She couldn't imagine anything more awful than a bunch of costumed adults drinking and playing stupid Halloween games in her house. She was not a party kind of person and it was not a party kind of house.

Belinda's face fell. "Oh, but I already gave out the invitations with my address." She looked a little heartbroken.

Relieved to be off the hook, Eve tried to cheer her up. "Your house is great for parties. You've got that big basement room and the great sound system."

Belinda perked up a little at the compliment and smiled. "You're right. My house will be fine. But next year you need to throw a party! Nothing more fun than a Halloween party at a haunted house."

"My house is not haunted," Eve insisted.

Belinda nodded condescendingly and patted her friend's arm. "Okay, Evie, whatever you say."

Later that night Eve relaxed on her lumpy yet comfortable living room sofa. Hazel and Sabrina curled up next to her, one on either side, both of them breathing deeply as they slept. With a hot cup of pumpkin spice tea in one hand and a worn copy of Dickens' Nicholas Nickleby that she had grabbed from the bookstore in the other, Eve was happily settled in for the night. The weather had cleared up today and though it was cold, almost freezing, the night sky was brilliant, thick and black and hung with a giant globe of a moon that lit up her trees and yard in a cool blue light.

Eve tried to focus on reading, but was continually interrupted by her thoughts. Foremost on her mind was Chip. This distressed her, as she believed she had spent far too much of her life dreaming and worrying and fussing over that man. This was nothing new. He had always gotten under her skin and this time was no different than when they were in school together so many years ago. What distressed her about the whole situation was she was fairly certain he hardly ever thought of her at all. All of her fantasies, good or bad, about meeting up with him at the Halloween party were just that, fantasies. It was entirely possible Chip wouldn't even show up at the party. He was famous for being aloof and noncommittal.

Eve sighed and took a sip of her tea. Sabrina rolled onto

her back and snuggled her face into Eve's thigh, asking for a tummy rub. Placing her book face down in her lap, Eve stroked the cat's rounded belly and Sabrina rewarded her with loud purring. A sound like boards creaking came from upstairs. Eve paused and listened.

The creaking stopped. It was the house settling, she was certain. This was an old house, over 130 years old. You can't live in an old house and not hear it occasionally creak and moan. She'd heard these sounds her whole life and never thought twice about them until now.

Sabrina rolled over and sat up, looking at Eve haughtily with her deep gold eyes. Her purring had stopped abruptly when Eve stopped stroking her belly. The cat butted her soft head against Eve's shoulder and pushed hard, trying to get her attention.

"Do you hear anything funny?" Eve asked Sabrina as she gently scratched behind the cat's ears. Sabrina answered with more purring. The commotion woke up Hazel who immediately wanted Eve's attention as well. Eve placed her tea on the side table and pet both cats to their great delight. She looked around her well-worn living room.

In addition to the lumpy green and yellow floral sofa where she sat, there was a giant, dark green, lumpy chair and an ottoman to match. The well made and roughly used heavy wood coffee table sat in the center of the room right in the middle of a large, blue and green Persian style rug. An antique secretary sat against one wall and the large original fireplace took up most of another wall. It wasn't usable anymore, because the chimneys were too delicate to risk starting a fire, but the deep green tiled hearth and antique wooden mantle with a long beveled mirror across the top were gorgeous even without a fire in the fireplace. Tall, fat candles were set up inside the fireplace and Eve lit them on nights like this with beautiful results. In addition to the furnishings there were various knick knacks, tons of framed photos, many of her and her father, and books, of course, books everywhere.

Eve smiled. Her home had never made her feel anything except warm and happy. There was no way it was haunted and, if it was, she had never noticed. All she could feel in this space was love, the love of her parents, the years she'd grown up here with her father reading to her and cooking and laughing, the comfort she'd felt returning home even after his death. It was a good house and she refused to let some goofy rumors make her think otherwise. In that moment, she categorically dismissed any thought of haunting. This was her home and Eve could never imagine anything bad ever happening to her here.

Chapter Six

"**A** field of ripe pumpkins under a bright blue sky is a true delight, wouldn't you say?" Atticus asked as they tromped across the rough surface of the harvested cornfield towards the pumpkin patch. The tall, green corn plants of summer were long gone and all that was left were the golden brown dried stalks and husks that had been chopped down and stripped of their corn by giant harvesters during their peak ripeness.

Owned by the Fischer family, this corn farm always set aside three acres to grow pumpkins and sell locally for Halloween. The pumpkins were dirt cheap compared to those sold in the store. The catch was, customers had to pick their purchases themselves and the closest anyone could get to the pumpkin patch was to park on the road and march over the uneven fields of corn surrounding it on all sides. Nobody was completely sure why the Fischers didn't plant their pumpkins along the road for easier access. Maybe it deterred late night teenage pumpkin thieves, or maybe they just thought people needed to get more exercise. Eve didn't mind, walking to the patch was part of what made it such a grand adventure.

She, Atticus, and his entire English class were on this adventure together today. The smell of turned earth, decaying corn plants and crisp, cold country air was a distinctly fall experience that she thoroughly enjoyed. From the looks on the kid's faces, they were enjoying it too. So was Atticus. The fresh air invigorated him, made him even more animated, and it turned the tip of his nose and tops of his ears pink, a look Eve was beginning to find charming.

"I see them!" He exclaimed, pointing for the other's benefit in the direction they needed to go. "Look at them, like happy orange orbs just waiting to be gathered up and taken home." He waved his long arms wildly towards the patch, encouraging his charges, "Run! Run, children, before they escape!"

Eve had to laugh as the children bounded off towards the patch in the distance, shouting and squealing. Under Atticus' direction these normally moody and sullen teenagers had turned into a gang of bright eyed, spirited explorers. On the bus ride from school, he'd led them all in silly songs until everyone was joining in the fun. He'd joked and sang and cajoled the whole lot of them into belly laughs. She couldn't remember the last time she had laughed that hard. The real delight, however, was seeing the kids lighten up and enjoy just being kids.

Atticus fell into step next to her, keeping one eye on his class from a distance.

"You're really wonderful with them," Eve said.

"Thank you." The pink from his ears spreading to his cheeks. "Coming from you that's quite a compliment."

"I'm sure my Dad would have approved of how you are with the kids." She was sure. The way Atticus engaged with this class reminded her more than just a little bit of her father, how he kept them entertained and learning all the time.

"I can't take all the credit," Atticus said. "I get very excited on field trips and I love anything orange, so for me today is a win-win!" He tilted his tousled red hair towards her and winked, making her laugh again. "And don't forget my new shoes!" He exclaimed, lifting his right foot up high in front of him so she could see his bright orange tennis shoes.

"How could I forget those shoes?"

He'd already shown them off three or four times on the bus ride only to receive protests and groans from the whole group. She couldn't tease him too much, she'd worn her own goofy Halloween sweatshirt with a giant, toothless pumpkin on the front to get in the spirit of the whole trip.

They continued walking, falling into a comfortable silence. She liked Atticus. He was funny and kind and she was glad he had taken over her father's class. Something about him made her feel like they'd known each other longer than only a few days.

"You still miss him, I imagine?" Atticus asked, breaking the friendly silence.

"My Dad?"

He nodded.

"Oh, yes, very much." A pang of grief went through her chest, but she was surprised to find she didn't start crying.

"What about your Mom?" Atticus asked.

"Oh, my Mom passed away when I was three," she responded. Atticus made a sympathetic noise, but didn't say anything. "How about you?" Eve asked, "Are your parents near here?"

Atticus shook his head 'no', "My Dad has never been around, I don't know anything about him." It was Eve's turn to be sympathetic. "And my Mom passed away about four years ago."

"I'm so sorry," Eve offered. Atticus nodded and looked into the distance as they walked.

"I have a younger sister who lives near here. That's why I transferred," he told her.

After that, there was nothing much to say, she knew. He completely understood her pain and learning this shifted something between them, it made walking quietly next to each other feel even more normal. She had an urge to reach out and touch his shoulder.

"Mr. Murphy! Mr. Murphy!" One of the boys, Simon, stood at the edge of the pumpkin patch about 30 feet away holding a bright orange pumpkin high over his head. "I found mine!"

"Excellent, Simon!" Atticus waved at the boy and turned to her, suddenly playful. "Ready to find your magic pumpkin, m'lady?" Eve nodded and Atticus gallantly offered his hand. She took it and he led her into the pumpkins like she was a princess and he was her knight in shining armor.

An hour later they were back at the school bus, laden with their round, orange bounty. Eve had realized that she couldn't buy a lot of pumpkins for Belinda's party because she didn't have any way to carry them all back to the bus. Atticus had offered to carry two for her and enlisted a few of the older boys who were only getting one for themselves to help her out by using their free arm to carry her extras. All in all she'd managed to procure six for Belinda's party and that seemed like enough.

The controlled chaos of loading two dozen teenagers and their pumpkins onto a school bus after romping outside in the fresh air was quite a sight to behold. Eve stood guard at the back end of the bus watching traffic. This road wasn't especially busy, but she felt like it was safer to make sure none of the kids stepped out past the edge of the bus, just in case. As she waited, a dark grey, shining sports car slowed down and pulled in to park behind them. The muffled thumping of music playing inside the car caught her attention. She peered at the driver who unexpectedly flashed a smile at her and instantly Eve knew who it was, Chip.

Chip turned off the engine and opened the door, emerging from the slick car looking like a man modeling a well cut suit, or the sports car itself, or a fancy brand of scotch in a magazine. He looked that good, like a scotch ad in a magazine.

"Chip," Eve greeted him, a flush of excitement making her smile like a goon.

"Hey," he said, meandering towards her.

Under his gaze she became acutely aware of her attire. She had on worn jeans, old tennis shoes and her sweatshirt, which, in addition to the smiling pumpkins, had the words 'Hocus Pocus' scrawled across the top. She hadn't put on much makeup and just swept her hair into a quick ponytail before heading to the school this morning. In short, she didn't feel quite prepared to face Chip Hendricks with his over the top, scotch ad good looks.

"You've been picking pumpkins?" He asked as he reached her, his voice was so deep and smoldering, even when he was talking about vegetables.

"Yeah." Eve had all but forgotten about the kids, the school bus, and even Atticus, when Chip got out of his car. "It's a school field trip."

"You volunteer at the school?" Chip looked over the back end of the bus and taking in the kids now visible in the windows, jumping and singing and generally being crazy.

"Oh, well not really." Eve couldn't find the words to explain exactly how she'd ended up here. "It's just a some-times thing...and I needed some pumpkins...for Belinda's party." Over explaining was a great way to look appealing, she thought to herself.

Chip grinned and, much to her chagrin, she found herself blushing.

"All right, Eve, we're rea—" Atticus jogged around the end of the bus and stopped short when he saw Chip. Chip didn't move from where he stood, which Eve suddenly noticed was quite close to her. He only turned his head and gave Atticus a once over, pausing for a beat on his very orange tennis shoes.

"Have you met each other?" Eve tried to break the ice. Chip didn't answer and Atticus shook his head 'no'. "Atticus, this is Chip Hendricks. We grew up together." She motioned towards Chip and Atticus stepped forward as if he might try to shake Chip's hand.

"I'm Atticus Murphy—" he started.

"He's the new English teacher," Eve interrupted. "He's teaching my father's class." She wanted Chip to understand why she was on this middle school field trip, but her words only added to the awkward vibe and nobody moved or said anything for a few moments. Before she knew what was happening, her nerves overtook her senses and she started explaining even harder, "I used to go on these trips with this class and Atticus, well the class really, invited me to come today, which is great because I needed some pumpkins for Belinda's party, but I couldn't carry them all back, and now that I think about it I don't know how I'm going to carry them all home because I walked to the school..." her voice trailed off a little and she let out a nervous laugh.

"I'll give you a lift," Chip said.

Eve's stomach did a little flip.

"Oh," she tried not to stammer. "You don't need to do that. I mean, following the bus all the way back to the school, isn't that a little out of your way?"

He chuckled and shook his head. "No, I mean I'll give you a lift from here. Put the pumpkins in the trunk." He pulled a key fob out of his pocket and pushed a button. The trunk on the sports car opened smoothly. "I insist," he added.

Eve blushed at her misunderstanding. Of course he didn't need to follow the school bus back to the school. She turned to Atticus, who remained quiet nearby.

"Well, um, I guess that would be okay?" She posed the question to Atticus. It was hard to ignore the look of disappointment that flashed across his face, but it disappeared in a nanosecond and turned to one of gracious acceptance. She was thankful to him for not making her feel guilty.

"Of course, no problem," Atticus said. "I'll just get your pumpkins for you."

A few minutes later she slid into the soft, leather seat of Chip's sports car. The seat was so low she could barely see over the dashboard, but she could see Atticus standing next to the bus. She waved at him and smiled, and he smiled and waved back. Then Chip started the car, revved the engine and pulled around the school bus, leaving it behind in a flash.

Chapter Seven

By the time Chip parked the car in front of her house, Eve felt dizzy. The swift power of the car, the heavy scent of fine leather and Chip's cologne, the strangeness of watching her home town whisk by through tinted windows, people she knew gawking as they sped past them towards her house, all of this made her head spin. The thing that she couldn't wrap her mind around, the thing that put her right over the edge into a lightheadedness, was her proximity to Chip and the way he was resting his hand on her thigh after each time he shifted the car into a different gear.

The first time he'd done it, she thought surely it must be an accident. This was a small car and maybe he didn't know where her leg was positioned. After the second time, she knew he was doing it on purpose and her heart pounded in her chest even as she stayed completely cool on the outside. She was riding in an expensive sports car with Chip Hendricks. He was taking her home. Of course it was no big deal that his hand lay on her thigh, moving slowly higher and higher as they got closer to their destination. No big deal at all.

Eve didn't know what to say, so she said nothing at all. She let her body sink into the leather seat that was built for comfort, looked out the window and let Chip's hand move where it wanted. Her body reacted strongly to his touch and she felt powerless to stop him.

He parked in front of her house. As the rumble of the engine stopped, she turned to look at him, determined to invite him in for a drink or dinner or something. He was already leaning towards her and his mouth clamped on hers before she could say a word.

Her first reaction was to pull away, but Chip slipped his free hand quickly around the nape of her neck, holding her to him. The hand on her thigh pushed further between her legs and gripped her firmly. His lips were hot and insistent, but not unpleasant. Once Eve was over the initial surprise of being kissed, she relaxed into it and the pleasure of the whole thing spread through her body. All of her sensations were alive with the feel of him, the smell of him, the plushness surrounding her and the hard warmth of his hand between her legs, his mouth against hers.

"Can I come in?" He pulled away from their kiss long enough to ask her the question in a husky whisper.

"Sure." Eve tried to remember if she'd left anything embarrassing laying around in her house. He came at her again for another kiss, this time pushing his tongue into her mouth. When she responded with her tongue, he made a little sound with his throat. She attempted to keep up with his fervor, but space in the car was cramped. "We'll have more room inside," she said during a breathing spell.

Chip laughed a little and leaned back in his seat. "Right, let's go."

As they walked up the path to the door, he put his hand on the small of her back, then let it slide down until it cupped her behind. Eve flushed and glanced up and down her street, wondering if any of her neighbors could see them.

"God, your house is creepy looking," Chip said as they walked up the front steps. The afternoon was turning to dusk and the clouds in the sky were no longer white and puffy, but grey and ominous, providing a rather gothic background for the peaked roof. The antique door loomed in front of them and Hazel and Sabrina sat in the front window, meowing at them excitedly. Still, Eve didn't think it was all that creepy.

"No it's not," she answered, a little offended.

"You have cats?" He asked, an air of disgust in his tone.

"Yes," Eve unlocked the front door. "You don't like cats?" He followed her into the foyer and pulled the door shut behind him.

"I'm allergic."

"Oh," said Eve. Right at that moment, Hazel and Sabrina rounded the corner from the living room into the foyer, meowing loudly and throwing themselves at the stranger, like always. "I'm sorry, I didn't know," Eve apologized.

"No problem," Chip responded, stiffening just a little as they wrapped around his ankles.

Any moment she knew they would start lovingly caressing him with their claws and probably snagging the pant legs of his suit. Chip sneezed. Eve cringed. The dizzying feeling of their magical ride home was dissipating quickly.

"Come on, girls." Eve scooped first Hazel then Sabrina up in her arms. She took the wriggling sister cats to the kitchen and dropped them gently on the floor. She closed the door as quickly as possible, barely getting it shut before Hazel stuck her head through the opening. The door kept the cats away from them, but it did nothing to stop their wailing at being locked up against their will.

Eve whirled around to return to Chip in the foyer, but cried out when she found him standing right behind her in the cramped hallway between her kitchen and her living room.

"I couldn't stay away," he said, leaning in to kiss her. But just before their lips touched he turned his face away quickly and sneezed again. Eve winced. She looked down at the front of her sweatshirt, which was now covered in black cat hair.

"I need to change," she said.

Chip put his hand behind her ear on the wall, right next to her parent's wedding picture, effectively blocking her escape. It was a sexy move, and a little unnerving. Eve couldn't tell if she liked it a lot or didn't like it at all.

"Or," he sniffled a few times as he slipped his other hand under her sweatshirt, caressing her stomach and pushing the sweatshirt up her body. "You could just take it off."

Eve's heart was pounding out of her chest. She was frozen. The feel of his warm, heavy hand sliding up her skin held her hostage. She gazed at him, Chip Hendricks, high school heartthrob. His thick, dark hair was disheveled and falling forward over his eyes. His beautiful lips were set in that crazy smirky sexy grin he had been giving her since they were kids, and she could tell he was moving in for another kiss. She made the decision right then that she was ready. This was Chip, after all. She had wanted him to want her for as long as she could remember. There was nothing more to think about, was there?

Chip's hand reached the sensitive area just below her bra and she inhaled sharply. That's when Eve felt something move against her back and there was a bump and a loud crash of glass shattering on the wood floor at their feet. Chip jumped back as Eve gave a cry of surprise. She looked down to see her parent's wedding photo smashed on the floor. The antique wood frame was broken in three pieces and the glass lay everywhere in shards.

"Oh, no!" Eve kneeled on the floor and began gingerly removing pieces of glass from the delicate face of the photo.

"I didn't touch it, I swear," Chip said, taking a few steps back. He sneezed loudly and cursed under his breath.

Big, fat tears welled up in Eve's eyes and she wiped them away with the sleeves of her sweatshirt so she could see what she was doing. How could she be so careless? The tears came full on now, she couldn't hold them back. It was just a photo, but she was overwhelmed at the prospect of it being destroyed.

Chip sneezed again, then he cleared his throat, "Maybe I should go now."

Eve didn't look up, she was too embarrassed. She just nodded and gave him a weak wave goodbye. As soon as she heard the door click shut, she sat down carefully next to the mess on the floor and let go with a good, old fashioned, sob.

When she finally cleaned everything up, her nose was red and her eyes were puffy. She let the sister cats out of the kitchen. They were incensed at their earlier treatment and let her know in no uncertain terms that they required a lot of love and attention to make up for her actions.

Eve sat on the couch with one cat on each side of her and inspected the wedding photo. She had been able to salvage it without damaging the main part, the actual images of her smiling, joyful parents. There was only slight damage on the bottom edge of the old picture and for that, Eve was very thankful. She placed the photo carefully on the coffee table. She would either fix the broken frame or find a replacement.

"That crisis was avoided, but can I fix the mess with Chip?" She asked the sister cats as she sat back and used both hands to rub behind their ears, one hand for each cat. Sabrina turned her wide, golden eyes to Eve and made a growling sound. Eve laughed, "What? You don't like him?" Sabrina turned away, refusing to give any further opinion. "What about you, Hazel?" Eve asked the smaller cat. Hazel looked at her and blinked a few times before putting her nose in the air and turning away. "Oh, I see," Eve said. "That's two 'no' votes." She sighed. "I'm talking to my cats again. Not a good sign."

Eve had to admit to herself, after the moment had passed, she was a little relieved nothing more had happened with Chip. Even though the incident had ended in embarrassment and near disaster. Now that it was over and she had time to think about it, she would be more comfortable postponing sleeping together, if they were going to sleep together, until they at least went out on a few dates. She wasn't really a hook up kind of girl.

"I'll just have to explain that to him," she told the sister cats. "If he's looking for a hook up, he'll need to look somewhere else." This made her feel better and she decided she would sleep on it and everything would look better in the morning. Just as she stood to go upstairs and get ready for bed, a thought struck her and she declared in dismay to her cat audience, "Belinda's pumpkins!"

Chapter Eight

The message on her voicemail was charming, full of nervous pauses and an apology for being so awkward. At the first sound of a male voice in the message, Eve's senses had perked up, thinking it was Chip. Almost immediately, however, she realized it was Atticus. Not that she was completely disappointed, but her heart sank a little bit knowing that Chip still hadn't contacted her after their make out fiasco yesterday.

On the other hand, Atticus had left the message to invite her to the Halloween Pageant at the school. This was a new development that the kids had pushed to put together. He told her in the message that they specifically wanted him to call and invite her to the event.

She took off early from the bookstore and walked to the school, enjoying the fine fall afternoon. She had decided to dress up a little today and was wearing her burnt orange and black plaid miniskirt with black tights and a matching burnt orange sweater. At least her outfit looked festive, even if she was feeling a little off kilter.

The school was abuzz with kids running around in

costume and their parents and siblings waiting in line outside the auditorium. Eve stayed near the wall, not diving into the merry crowd. She'd never been one for large groups, preferring to stay on the perimeter and people watch. Eve saw Mrs. Runyon and waved 'hello'. She also saw the principal, Gary Sunder, and many of the teachers that she knew were friends of her father.

Then there was Atticus.

Taller than almost everyone there, he stood behind a table where several of the kids were handling ticket and refreshment sales. Like all school events, the Halloween Pageant was also a fundraiser and there were Rice Krispie treats, chocolate brownies and popcorn balls dyed orange with food coloring and stuffed with candy corns, all available for 50 cents each. Atticus wore a light orange dress shirt, a purple tie with a cartoon of a fat black cat down the front and jeans. She couldn't see from where she was, but she guessed he also had on his bright orange tennis shoes. His collar was unbuttoned and the tie was loose, the sleeves of his shirt were pushed up to his elbows. His arms seemed long and leanly muscled as she watched him point and direct, answering several questions at once from different directions and generally being involved and competent.

She liked watching Atticus in his teacher role. He had such good humor and being in charge made him shine.

He saw her, locked his eyes on hers and broke into a smile so wide she couldn't help but smile back. He bent down and said something to one of the ticket salesmen then stepped on and over two empty chairs that were blocking his exit. Making his way through the crowded waiting area, Atticus kept his eyes trained on her, the same beaming smile on his face. It seemed like a warm, glowing spotlight was on her as he got closer. She felt her cheeks heat up under the attention.

Then he was there, standing very close because the crowd

behind him didn't allow much room. She looked up into his face, his beard was nicely trimmed and his red hair was artfully tousled. He smelled warm and spicy, with a hint of mint. He smiled down at her, his blue eyes bright and happy.

"You're here," he said.

"I'm here!" She made a 'ta-da' movement with her hands.

"You look very nice in orange," he said.

"So do you," she responded. Without thinking, Eve reached up and flipped his tie with her finger. "Nice tie."

Something moved between them, an electrical current, a moment of intensity that was palpable. She saw it on his face and felt it in her own body. His blue eyes darkened with it. For a split second Eve was positive Atticus was going to bend down and kiss her right here in the waiting room of the school auditorium. He didn't. Instead he let his gaze move to her mouth for just a moment before it flicked back up to her eyes. Then she felt his hand take hers.

"Come with me." He led her through the crowd towards the door leading to the backstage of the auditorium.

She followed Atticus through the door, into a narrow, dark hall then behind the heavy curtains that stretched high into the catwalk above. There were excited teens everywhere, some donned headsets and were dressed from head to toe in black, some were obviously in costume wearing stage makeup, some of them wore street clothes and it was hard to determine if they were supposed to be there or if they had just snuck back to take part in the festive chaos of the pageant.

"She's here!" Atticus announced to anyone in earshot. The excited conversations ebbed for a moment as all of the students looked at Eve. She lifted a hand in 'hello', not sure why Atticus felt the need to show her off to the whole cast and crew. "Who would like to show her to her seat?" He asked. A gangly, dark haired youth with a nose he had not yet grown into, wearing a jacket he'd outgrown two years ago, stepped forward.

"I will, Mr. Murphy," the youth said. His voice was far too deep for his face and body.

"My seat?" Eve asked, confused.

Atticus looked at her, his eyes twinkling with the secret. "The kids have something special prepared." Eve started to ask what this was all about, when the gangly young man gallantly offered her his arm. "James will show you to your seat, Miss St. Claire," Atticus said formally. He squeezed her hand warmly as he passed her off to James. She politely took the boy's arm and let him lead her out onto the stage, down the stairs that led into the half filled audience and to a chair that was one of four marked off with orange crepe paper located front row, center stage.

James cleared the crepe paper from one of the chairs and swept his arm dramatically towards it, indicating she should sit down.

"Thank you," she said.

"You're very welcome, Madame. Enjoy the show." James gave her a half bow and bounded back onto the stage, disappearing behind the curtain.

The theatre behind her filled quickly as the crowd from the waiting area continued to file in and choose their seats. A headset wearing teen walked onto the stage and tested the mic that stood on a stand in the middle. The spotlights went through a series of tests and the seated audience buzzed with conversation. Principal Sunder and his wife were shown by James to two of the crepe paper chairs, which left one open next to Eve. She wondered who was supposed to sit there. She could take a guess, but decided not to let her imagination get away with her, she would just wait and see.

A few minutes went by as Eve made small talk about the weather with Mrs. Sunder. The house lights blinked off and on and a young girl's voice came over the speakers asking that everyone take their seats as the Halloween Pageant was about to begin. The audience obeyed, conversations tapered off and almost everyone got settled. Still the seat next to Eve remained empty.

Then it was time. The house lights turned off, leaving them in total darkness for a few seconds. A spotlight flicked on, illuminating Atticus standing at the microphone.

"Good evening," Atticus spoke into the mic, his voice booming through the room. "Thank you for coming." He looked into the unlit audience as he continued, "Tonight we are happy to present the very first annual Halloween Pageant at Fielding Middle School." A ripple of applause and a few random hoots from students rose from the crowd. "This is an event that the students voted for, planned and are performing today," Atticus dropped his gaze so he was looking directly at Eve in the front row, "in loving memory of Albert St. Claire. We hope you enjoy the performance."

Eve gasped at the mention of her father. Atticus stepped away from the mic as applause and cheers filled the room. He walked quickly across the stage, hopped off the front and landed right in front of Eve. He sat in the chair next to her and even though they were virtually in the dark, she could feel his smile. She blinked back tears.

James approached the microphone from backstage. A few kids shouted his name from the audience and he waved sheepishly in their general direction. He adjusted the microphone to his height and pulled a piece of paper out of his too small jacket pocket.

"I am going to read from this cause I don't want to mess it up," he said into the mic, more cheers from his buddies in the crowd. He waved them off, cleared his throat and began, "School sucks." Laughter erupted from the audience. James waited for it to quiet down then began again, "School sucks."

He held up a finger to stop any reaction. "Not always...just sometimes. But there are teachers who have a gift for making school fun." Here he grinned at the audience. "Not always...just sometimes." More laughter. "Seriously, though, sometimes you get a teacher who makes learning interesting, that makes you look forward to going to class and even makes homework exciting. For many of us here at Fielding Middle School, Mr. St. Claire was that teacher."

Eve's heart swelled with pride and she had to swallow hard to hold down her tears.

"Why Halloween?" James continued, gesturing towards a backdrop that lit up behind him showing a huge moon with the silhouette of a witch on a broom, a few giant jack-o'lanterns and an old house that looked a lot like hers painted to look like it was in the distance. "Mr. St. Claire loved Halloween. Even more than Christmas! He taught English and he loved stories. He loved the scary ones and the sad ones and the funny ones. He wasn't afraid to let us write things that weren't pretty and happy. He taught us to not be afraid of anything and to read and learn and express ourselves in whatever ways worked for us."

Tears rolled down Eve's cheeks. She couldn't stop them. She felt Atticus pat her hand with his and she turned her palm up so she could hold his hand and share this moment with him.

"But more than anything," James said, putting his paper back in his pocket. He knew the next bit by heart. "We dedicate this Halloween Pageant to the memory of Mr. St. Claire, because the biggest reason he loved Halloween was he believed, and he wanted us to believe, that life is full of magic."

And with that, the pageant began.

It was brilliant. There were paper mâché pumpkins, witches and warlocks, ghosts and goblins, a group of robots for some reason, skits, jokes, singing performances by the school choir and a rather frightening reading by James himself of The Tell Tale Heart. Eve took it all in with enormous pleasure. Atticus did too, and he held her hand until it was time to applaud.

Afterward, her heart was full in many ways. Memories of her father wrapped together with scenes from the pageant and the powerful feeling of having been raised by such a good man lifted her spirits. Her hand still felt the warmth of Atticus' touch and she allowed a sparkle of romantic possibility to flicker across her mind. He was attractive and fun and kind, but was she interested in him romantically? Was he interested in her? She wore a quiet smile as she approached her house, ready to spend some time with the sister cats and think about her day. As she got closer, her smile faded.

Six orange pumpkins had been placed in a line by her front door. Belinda's pumpkins.

Eve looked around for signs of Chip or his car, but didn't see any. Her mood fell and she was inexplicably bothered by the sight of the perfectly innocent pumpkins. Was he trying to be cute? Or sexy? Was he trying to seduce her or dump her? She didn't know and, what was most confusing, she found that she didn't really care.

Chapter Nine

Halloween fell on Saturday this year, which always made for the most fun possible. Kids were out of school and able to attend whatever festivities they desired and go trick-or-treating until as late as they desired, because there was no school in the morning. Most adults had the weekend free, so their parties tended to be more boisterous than a weekday Halloween party. Plus, they had all day to decorate and get their costumes in order.

That's what Eve was doing. It was just before noon on Saturday and she was getting ready to go to Belinda's house and help her decorate for the big Halloween blast. The day was a perfect Halloween day, overcast and windy with the hint of a storm brewing, exactly what you would expect to conjure up some trouble.

Trouble wasn't something Eve was hoping for, however. She had some trepidation about seeing Chip at the party. He still hadn't called her or come by after dropping off the pumpkins at her door. She wasn't sure how she was supposed to interpret his behavior, but she knew it put her a little on edge. There was nothing she could do about it now, though.

Belinda was expecting her to be at the party and Eve had no real excuse not to go. She owed it to her friend, even if Chip showed up or didn't show up and ruined her evening one way or another.

Eve had packed everything she needed to change into her costume, which Belinda had finished sewing for her and had ready at her house. All that was left was to load the pumpkins into her car. She was saying goodbye to the sister cats in the kitchen where they'd just eaten a special treat of tuna fish when both of them perked their ears and ran to the living room window, meowing like crazy.

"What is it?" She asked them, following them to the window to see what had grabbed their attention. She pulled back the curtain just in time to see Atticus climbing her front steps. He wore jeans and a brown sport coat, an orange and black striped scarf wrapped jauntily around his neck and, of course, those orange sneakers. He saw her in the window and waved, holding up a book for her to see. A tiny thrill shimmered through her and she went to the door to let him in, the sister cats were already there.

"Happy Halloween!" Atticus greeted her, beaming. Hazel immediately leapt into his arms like she had the first time she'd met him. "Hello, you beautiful beasties!" He scooped Sabrina up so he could hold both purring cats. Eve watched in amazement.

"I've never seen them take to someone like they've taken to you," she said, stepping back so Atticus could come in the house.

"Well, I must admit, today I'm carrying a secret weapon." He handed her the book he was carrying. It was a well worn edition, covered in a blue, cloth like material with gold lettering across the front that read 'To Kill a Mockingbird'. "I brought that for you. I found it in the bottom drawer of your Dad's desk and thought you might want it."

Eve took the book and smoothed her hand over the cover. "To Kill a Mockingbird," she laughed in surprise at the coincidence of Atticus sharing the name of the main character. "How ironic!"

"I know, that's what I thought," Atticus said with a chuckle. He maneuvered the sister cats around in his arms so he could pull a small bag out of his jacket pocket. Hazel and Sabrina started purring so hard Eve could almost feel the vibrations from where she stood. "And this," he turned the bag so she could see it, "Is my secret weapon. I got these for my sister's cat. I'm going by there tomorrow. I thought maybe you wouldn't mind if I gave your beauties some." The bag read 'Catnip Puffs' and the sister cats were climbing all over the poor man trying to get at it.

"Yes, that's fine," Eve laughed at their crazed reaction. "You better give it to them soon, before they eat you alive!"

After he distributed a few puffs on the living room floor for the cats to attack and tucked the rest of the bag neatly back into his jacket pocket, Eve invited him to have a cup of tea. She figured she had time for a cup of tea before leaving for the party. Standing at the kitchen counter, Atticus took note of the remains of the picture frame that lay there waiting to be glued.

"Have a little accident?" He asked.

"Yes," Eve felt suddenly uncomfortable talking about the picture falling off the wall with Atticus, given what she'd been doing when it fell. She pulled the kettle off of the stove and poured hot water into their mugs. Atticus picked up the largest piece of the picture frame.

"Next time you could try taking out the screws before pulling it off the wall. That way the frame won't break," he offered, inspecting the back of the broken frame.

"I didn't pull it off," Eve said, blushing a little. "I just, kind of, bumped it."

"Really?" Atticus peered at the screws sticking out the back of the frame. "Is this the frame from your parent's wedding picture?" She nodded and he stepped into the small hallway holding the broken frame up next to where it had detached from the wall. "Hmm," he mumbled to himself, looking puzzled.

"What is it?" Eve joined him in the cramped hallway and immediately became very aware of how close their bodies were to touching. She had wild mixed feelings, remembering kissing Chip right here in this spot, and experiencing a tiny thrill from standing so near Atticus with his warm, spicy scent.

"It's just..." Atticus looked once again at the back of the picture frame and at the holes in the wall where it had hung, "I don't know how it could have possibly fallen off with these screws put in this way. It looks like it was very sturdy. Normally you would have to yank on it with two hands to pull this kind of mounting out of the wall like this."

"You would?" Eve hadn't taken time to look over the damage yet. She'd assumed the picture had hung like a normal picture on a wire or hanging on a single nail in the wall. She inspected what Atticus was looking at more closely. There were two long screws that had been screwed straight through the top two corners of the frame and into the wall. Sturdy. Very sturdy.

"Well, maybe it was the old plaster," Atticus shrugged. "Do you need any help hanging this back up?" He turned towards her when he asked and their faces were very near. He waited for her to answer, and while he waited his blue eyes wandered to her lips and back. Eve was frowning, still wondering what could have made the picture fall the other evening. She hadn't touched it and Chip, even if he had bumped it, which he denied, definitely hadn't grabbed hold of it and pulled with two hands. His hands had been other places. She noticed Atticus was still waiting for a reply.

"Oh, no thank you," she said, letting her eyes wander down his jaw line to his mouth. She noticed how nicely his beard was trimmed and felt a tingle up her spine. "I think I'm going to buy another one." Because they were so close, she spoke softly. She saw something flicker through his eyes. Desire?

"Was the picture damaged?" He asked, his own voice low and a little husky.

"No."

"That's good."

They stood there for a few moments, the air crackling between them. Eve wondered what it would be like to kiss him. Then Atticus seemed to make a decision. He took a deep breath and pushed gently past her back into the kitchen.

"I'm glad nothing got ruined," he said as he carefully placed the broken frame back on the counter.

Eve remained in the small hallway, breathless, trying to compose herself. Something caught the corner of her eye and she turned to see the sister cats sitting in the opening to the living room, staring at her. They were both completely still, their eyes glowing yellow, their tails flicking in unison behind them. They had the same odd expressions, as if they were asking her a silent question.

"What?" Eve whispered at them. Then Hazel looked at Sabrina and Sabrina looked back. They came to a mutual decision, turned their backs on her, and trotted back into the living room. "Crazy cats," Eve muttered to herself.

"Do you have plans for Halloween?" Atticus asked her from the kitchen. Eve returned to answer him.

"Yes, I'm going to a party my friend is throwing," she

answered. She wondered if Belinda had ever gotten around to inviting Atticus to the party.

His face fell a bit. "So you're busy all night."

"Yes, mostly, why?"

Atticus fiddled with his cup of tea nervously, avoiding her gaze. Then he took a deep breath and lifted his eyes to meet hers. "I was wondering if you might want to go to a movie with me tonight? Scary or not scary, whatever you like. Kind of a Halloween...date."

"Oh." The tingling returned to her neck and shoulders. "I can't, I–" Just then, a heavy gust of wind hit the house and the front door blew open. The door banged against the wall and dried leaves swept into the foyer. "For heaven's sake," Eve exclaimed. "I thought I shut that."

She rushed into the foyer to close the door, Atticus right behind her. He ducked past her to grab the door and stood in the doorway as if to leave. Dismayed at the idea of Atticus going as well as missing out on a Halloween date with him, Eve took hold of the door as well.

"You don't have to go," she said.

"It's okay," he answered. "You've got plans. Maybe another time." He stepped backwards through the door onto the front porch. Giving her a quick wave he said in an overly cheery tone, "Have a Happy Halloween, Eve."

Then he was walking quickly away and another cold wind blew through her front door. Eve felt a pang of regret. Why didn't she invite him to the party? Why didn't she stop him from leaving? The way his shoulders had hunched down and he shoved his hands in his pockets as he walked away made him look sad and lonely and made her feel like a jerk.

Turning back into her house and shutting the door firmly, Eve saw the sister cats sitting squarely in the wide doorway that went to the living room. Their catnip puffs lay ignored on the floor behind them. Both of them looked at her with disapproving glares.

"What do you want me to do? Tackle him?" Eve asked them, exasperated. The sister cats turned their black, furry rumps to her and stalked away.

Chapter Ten

Belinda's house was a bustle of energy, much like her personality. There were decorations to put up, snacks to prepare, punch to mix, music to set up on her sound system and when they were finished with that, they had to get dressed in their costumes.

Belinda, true to her word, had made brilliant alterations to her thrift store finds and Eve thought they both looked the part of the witches from Wicked. Belinda brushed glitter onto her face in her upstairs bathroom while Eve inspected her green makeup options.

"Don't forget your hat," Belinda reminded her. Eve took up the black pointed hat and placed it on her head, studying her reflection. She had curled her long, dark hair upon Belinda's suggestion and with much of her friend's help. "No need to be an unattractive witch," her friend had said. Belinda could work magic with hair just like she did with clothes and seeing her wavy locks tumbling out from under the black hat and around her shoulders, Eve was happy with the look. Her dress was form fitting, fairly low cut and had an abundance of black silk and taffeta strips attached to her wrists so when she moved, she fluttered. The only part about her costume she wasn't crazy about was the green makeup.

"You don't think my eyes will be too pale if my skin is green, do you?" Eve asked.

"I thought of the color of your eyes when I bought it, which is why I got the paler green. I think it will make them brighter," Belinda answered. "Just try it, if you really hate it you have time to wash it off." The doorbell rang and Belinda finished her bright pink lipstick quickly. "Trick-or-treaters are starting! The red lipstick is for you." Belinda pointed at a tube of lipstick next to the green glitter makeup and disappeared out the door.

"May as well go for it," Eve said to her reflection. She dipped her fingers into the pot of green makeup and smeared it on her cheeks. By the time she was done, every inch of her face and neck and ears was a pale, shimmering green. Her lips were a beautiful poppy red and she silently blessed Belinda for her fashion sense. The color of the green did bring out her pale blue eyes, making them a deeper blue/green color. Eve took one last look in the full-length mirror. She looked transformed into someone else, which was what a costume was supposed to do, wasn't it?

Downstairs, the party had already started. When Eve descended the stairs it was not into the suburban home she had entered earlier in the day. Belinda's house was now a full on Halloween blowout. All of the best music, including Monster Mash, Ghostbusters and Time Warp, blasted over the sound system. The fog machines were working double time to keep a mystical layer of fog floating around the feet of the guests who continued to stream through the front door. The rooms were dark except for glowing white globes that looked like moons and strings of purple and orange lights hung along the walls. Everyone was decked out in full costumes and Eve was continually surprised at not recognizing old friends until they revealed who they were as she walked through the crowd. She found Belinda by the punch bowl that was flowing over with dry ice mist.

"This is great!" Eve shouted to Belinda over the music.

"You look fantastic!" Belinda responded, "The green looks really cool in this light. And doesn't it make your eyes look brilliant?" Belinda was obviously delighted with her costume creation.

"Yes, you were right." Eve took a cup of the punch Belinda offered. "Did you invite Atti–Mr. Murphy?" Eve asked, wondering if she might see him tonight after all.

Belinda continued pouring punch into cups, "No, I didn't. I don't really know him and I never ran into him this week. Should I have?"

"No," Eve tried to seem nonchalant. "Not really, I guess."

"Have you seen Chip?" Belinda asked. Eve's stomach tightened at the question. She shook her head 'no', not sure she wanted to find him. "Me neither," Belinda said, her eyebrows screwing into a knot.

Eve shrugged, "It doesn't matter, this is a great party with or without him!" She lifted her cup and toasted Belinda's in a toast. She took a drink and immediately felt the burn of vodka in her throat. She coughed.

"It's spiked," Belinda told her, grinning before taking a big swig of her own drink.

Between the spiked punch, the loud music and the crowd of dancing characters that ranged from a giant Winnie the Pooh to a sexy devil lady who by day sold car insurance at the local State Farm, this was definitely an epic Halloween event. Eve couldn't think of the last time she'd been to such a wild party, if ever. After chatting with some of her friends and downing a couple of glasses of punch, Eve took up her favorite position at any party, in the most out of the way place she could find. Nestled into the darkest corner, she perched on a stool, munched steaming hot cheese puffs from a paper plate and people watched.

Not long after taking her place as resident wallflower, Eve felt a melancholy wash over her, a sad kind of loneliness that she couldn't explain. She popped the last cheese puff into her mouth and chewed it thoughtfully. For one thing, the number of couple's costumes in the room was a little depressing. She saw a sailor and a mermaid, Danny and Sandy from Grease, Barbie and Ken, Little Red Riding Hood and the Big Bad Wolf, a priest and a nun and Wesley and Buttercup from The Princess Bride. This last one made her especially moody, such a romantic story. She wondered what Atticus was doing right now. Had he found someone else to take on a Halloween date? That thought made her even more depressed.

"Do you want to dance?" The unmistakable gravelly voice came from the darkness beside her. She jumped, losing her balance on the stool. A hand clad in a black glove grabbed her arm to steady her. "Whoa, I didn't mean to scare you."

Eve looked up into the face of...Batman.

She peered into the mask, trying to see the man's eyes before she blurted out his name. It was no use, there wasn't enough light and she realized she had drank her punch a little too fast and could not see completely clearly at the moment. She could make out the man's mouth through the opening in the mask, however, and after a few moments of concentration she recognized the smirky grin.

"Chip?"

"Do you want to dance?" He asked again, moving his hand under her elbow to guide her to the middle of the living room where a strange blend of characters were bouncing and gyrating to Michael Jackson's 'Thriller'.

"Sure," she said, even though she didn't think he could hear her answer. They were already halfway into the dancing mob.

Batman, or Chip—she was pretty sure it was Chip—had pretty good moves. The music and the punch got to her and Eve lost herself in dancing. She was no longer Eve St. Claire, bookworm, cat lady in the making. She was a sexy witch and she was dancing with Batman. She was, in fact, dirty dancing with Batman now that he'd grabbed her around the waist and pulled her into him. She found it easy to match his rhythmic pelvic moves and when the song finished, they were almost in a full embrace. The music shifted to a slow song, Love Song for a Vampire, Eve recognized it immediately.

"Stay," Chip said when she started to back away. He took her by the waist and she wrapped her arms around his neck and they swayed to the music. Eve saw Belinda notice them from the other side of the room. Belinda's mouth dropped open, then she lifted her hands and gave Eve two thumbs up.

The rest of the night she was his. Chip stayed by her side, bringing her snacks and refilling her punch several times. He stood by her as they made small talk with other guests and they danced with each other exclusively. Eve felt dizzy from the attention. She felt claimed, like they were one of those couples that had dressed to match each other at the party. He took off his mask so he could talk and he was easily the handsomest man in the room. She blushed under his attention, letting him hold her close and kiss her neck during more slow dances. After a while she had drank too much and told him so. He asked if she wanted to go home and said he would drive. She agreed.

Eve found herself once again sunk deep in the leather passenger seat of Chip's car. The wind had picked up and briefly cleared the hazy clouds so there was just cold, black sky where the giant moon hung. Perfect for Halloween. She turned to say something to Chip about it and took in his Batman outfit, then thought about her own witch costume and green face. She touched her head, she still had her hat on.

The idea of what they must look like driving around in his sleek sports car tickled her funny bone so completely that she burst out laughing.

"What?" Chip asked as he shifted gears and placed his hand proprietarily on her thigh.

Eve started to answer, then looked down at his hand and was reminded of the fiasco of the last time he took her home. His sneezing fit and the way her parent's wedding picture had mysteriously fallen off the wall and interrupted them. She started laughing even harder. She couldn't stop, and after a few minutes Chip grew annoyed.

"What is so funny?" He asked, turning onto Pennsylvania, her street.

"Next stop, the haunted house!" Eve blurted out, sending herself into another bout of hysterical laughter. She had a blurred idea that perhaps she had drank too much punch and tried to explain to Chip, "I had too much spooky brew!" She heard the slur in her words and collapsed into the door handle, giggling uncontrollably.

Chip didn't say anything. They pulled up to her house and he helped her out of the car then to her front door. The old house loomed dark and empty next to them. She had forgotten to leave a lamp on in the living room. Eve fumbled in her purse for her keys, still chuckling quietly, when a sudden cold wind whipped by them, whisking her hat off of her head.

"Whoops!" She cried as she lunged for it, dropping her keys in the process.

"I'll get it," Chip said. He sounded exasperated and it took him a few long minutes and more than a little effort of feeling around the porch to find both lost items. Finally, he stood up and handed her the keys and the hat. "Can we get inside? This costume is flimsy and that wind is cold."

Eve bit her lip and didn't make any comment, even

though the idea of Batman shivering on her porch was really, really funny. She tried to get the key in the hole three different times, but missed. Finally, Chip put his flimsy, fake Batman gloved hand over hers and put the key in, turning the lock. Eve pushed on the door, but nothing happened. It stayed stubbornly closed. She pushed it again, nothing. Chip tried the door and it wouldn't budge.

"Give me the key, maybe it's still locked," he said brusquely.

Eve handed him the key and watched as he used it to lock and unlock the door several times, pushing it each time to try and open it, to no avail. The chilling wind continued to blow and Chip sighed and grunted in irritation.

"It doesn't normally get stuck," Eve explained, half apologizing, half wondering what was wrong with the door.

"Are you sure this is the unlocked position?" Chip asked. Eve checked the key placement and nodded 'yes' earnestly. "Stand back," Chip commanded. She stepped back and watched him walk to the edge of the porch, turn around, lower his shoulder and run at the door, slamming his shoulder into it with a loud bang before bouncing backwards.

"Oh!" She exclaimed, "Be careful." Even as she said it she had to giggle at the look of him getting thrown backwards.

"I felt it move," he said with confidence, stepping back to the edge of the porch to try again. All in all, Chip ran at her door four times. The first three ended in the same banging sound and with him being thrown back, unable to move the door. The fourth time the door opened, Eve saw it, or at least that's what she thought she saw. She wasn't completely sure, because it seemed to open just moments before Chip hit it with his shoulder. It sort of slipped open a tiny crack all on its own. She tried to tell him, but it was too late, he was already in full on attack mode and he hit the slightly open door with all of his weight, slamming it so hard that it crashed against the inside wall and his momentum hurled him into the foyer where he slipped and fell, sprawling onto the floor.

Eve ran in after him, afraid he might have hurt himself. A bitter cold wind followed her, making the strands of the silk and taffeta on her costume flutter madly. She flipped on the light to see Chip laying face down on the floor, his arms and legs still spread wide, his Batman cape twisted in disarray around him. She also saw the sister cats placed in odd positions, glaring at Chip with frightful anger. Hazel stood at the top of the staircase, her back arched, her tail shooting straight up behind her, yellow eyes glowing. And Sabrina, she was almost directly in front of Chip's head, her front and back legs set wide apart, her back hunched with her jet black hair sticking up straight all along her spine, making her look even bigger than her already large size. Her great yellow eyes were slits and she emitted a terrible, guttural, growling sound. It made a shiver go down Eve's spine.

"Holy shit!" Chip shouted as he struggled to get up, his tangled cape causing him to slip and slide across the foyer floor before he finally managed to stand. He stared at Sabrina as he straightened his cape. The cat continued to growl. "What in the hell is the matter with your cat?"

"Nothing...I don't know," Eve answered, surprised at the cat's behavior, but even more bothered at Chip's angry reaction. "They're just cats. We scared them. It's probably the full moon."

Chip scoffed and ran his hand through his hair, trying to smooth it after his tumble. "What, because you're a witch for Halloween you think you know all about the full moon?"

Eve didn't like his tone. It was sarcastic and belittling.

"You think you can break down doors because you're dressed like Batman?" She quipped.

"Excuse me for trying to help you," he replied. Sabrina growled again. "Are you gonna get those cats locked up bef—"

suddenly Chip opened his mouth into a wide yawn that went on forever and ended in a massive sneeze. Both cats bolted. Eve watched in shocked curiosity as Chip sneezed five more earth shattering times. Tears streamed from his eyes, his nose was bright red and he had to lean against the wall to keep his balance.

"Are you all right?" She asked.

"No, I'm not all right," he said. "I just wanted to have a little fun tonight, get in a little action before I head home on Monday and this is what I get for my trouble?"

Eve felt her hackles rise, just like the sister cats. She was still a little drunk, but she wasn't too drunk to misunderstand his meaning. She was his Halloween hook up. He was going back home to Chicago in two days and he only took her home tonight because he wanted to get laid.

"You're going back to Chicago on Monday?" Eve asked icily.

"Yes," Chip answered with a scowl. "Thank God. I can't stand this stupid town. I don't know how anyone still lives here. The whole place is full of losers."

There was such disdain in his voice Eve was almost at a loss for words. Almost. She stepped to the door and swung it all the way open, gesturing outside with a wide sweep of her arm.

"Then you better go home and get packing," she told him.

Chip Hendricks, her high school crush, teenage heart-throb of their town, wearing a cheap Batman outfit and suffering from watery eyes and extreme sniffles, stood in her foyer with his mouth agape.

"You're not serious," he said. Apparently, Chip wasn't familiar with rejection, especially from a 'loser' in this 'stupid town'.

"I'm dead serious," Eve told him, letting her eyes narrow like Sabrina's. Another cold wind blasted through the door as if to emphasize her words. He gave her one last look of disgust, then stormed out the door to his car and out of her life, hopefully forever.

Eve stood at the door with her shoulders back and her head held high, watching him drive away.

"Good riddance," she said, expecting Hazel and Sabrina to hurry to her side in support. But they didn't. In fact, they were nowhere to be seen.

Eve's stomach dropped with a sickening realization. It was midnight on Halloween, her front door had been wide open for several minutes while she and Chip argued, and the sister cats were gone.

Chapter Eleven

It had been stupid to leave the house without a coat. Eve knew that now. Not only that, but her purse and her phone sat on the small table in her foyer where she'd put them after Chip fell through the door. She'd been in such a frenzy of worry she hadn't thought anything through, just ran outside looking for Hazel and Sabrina. She'd hoped to find them exploring in the wooded area behind her house, or maybe frolicking with other cats in her neighbor's yards, or maybe even on a wild adventure in Sander's Park whose entrance was just four blocks from her house.

She hadn't found them in any of those places. As she searched, calling their names, the futility of finding two completely black cats in the middle of the night sunk in. The wind had picked up and the giant, glowing moon looked a lot creepier than it had earlier in the evening. Thick clouds were moving over it, giving it an eerie quality and quickly blotting out its light. The trick-or-treaters and their families had gone home a long time ago. It was too late for little kids to be out. All of the scariest stories she'd ever read flew through her mind as she trudged through the park. Trees swayed, moaning in the wind, their bare limbs scratching against each other. Houses everywhere were dark, shuttered against the storm and maybe against the frightening forces of Halloween night. Not one jack-o-lantern had been left glowing on anyone's stoop. Eve felt utterly alone. It took all of her concentration to control the icy fear that crept up from her belly.

That's when it started to rain.

Cold splinters of water carried by the wind whipped into her face. She stopped, turning around slowly to orient herself. In her frantic searching, she'd lost track of how far she'd gone. She was on the far side of Sander's Park now. It was almost a thirty minute walk home from where she stood and the sister cats were nowhere in sight. Her car was still at Belinda's, whose house was even farther away. Fat, hot tears welled up in her eyes and started rolling down her face. She had to go home without Hazel and Sabrina, and it was her own fault.

She'd been such a fool. There were so many red flags that she should have noticed with Chip. She'd ignored every one of them, because she'd been, what? Flattered by his attention? Finally getting a shot with her high school crush? Ridiculous. Even her beautiful old house had given her a sign that Chip wasn't right for her, and she hadn't listened. And this is what she got for it, missing cats and a long walk home in the rain in the middle of the night. There was nothing to do but give up for now. The sister cats were nowhere nearby and whether the fear she felt in her belly was from something real or something imagined, she wanted to go home.

Eve's hat was already pulled down hard around her ears so she wouldn't lose it in the wind again. Her witch costume wasn't the cheap, thin costume you might buy in a store, but it still wasn't terribly warm and it definitely wasn't water-proof. She wrapped her arms around her body to try and control her shivering and made towards home as the rain began in earnest.

By the time she got within a half block of her driveway, Eve was soaked to the bone. Her witch hat and dress were soggy, as was her hair and shoes. Though the wind had died down now that the rain was going full force, her shivering was even more out of control because she was so wet.

Her house was completely dark, as was every house along her street. Even the street lamps were out. Her heart beat wildly at the creepy possibilities this total blackout held on a Halloween night. Of course, logically, it was probably just a powerful outage, but still. Through the rain she saw a faint light flash across her front porch. She paused for a moment, trying to remember if she'd locked her front door in her rush to leave, then cursing silently when she realized her keys were inside her purse, which was inside the house.

A form moved on the porch. Eve took a step back. The form was large enough to be a man, but through the rain and without any light coming from the moon or anywhere else, it was difficult to tell what it was.

"Eve?" A man's voice sounded from the porch, then the light came again, a flashlight. It swept across the ground in front of her then across her dress and into her face, blinding her for a moment. She shielded her eyes with her hand.

"Hey!" She shouted, trying to sound less scared than she felt.

"Sorry." The light shone on the ground then swept up to fall on the form holding it. She was right, it was a man. It was Atticus. "It's me!" He waved one hand at her. "Your front door was open..." his voice trailed off as she made her way up the front steps and he got a better look at her. "Jeez, what happened? Are you all right?"

"I'm j-j-just cold," she stammered, relieved as he grabbed her arm pulling her under the small porch roof then swung the front door open and led her inside. She was dripping and shaking and crying. Atticus' flashlight lit the foyer sporadically as he moved. He shut the door behind her.

"Do you have candles? The power's out," he asked.

Eve nodded, pointing towards the kitchen. "D-d-drawer by the sink."

He disappeared and she could hear him moving around in the kitchen. She took off her shoes, grateful for the warm, dry house. She imagined she heard a muffled meow from upstairs and felt another ache of grief over the sister cats being lost out in this storm. Atticus returned, carrying a lit candle in front of him. The candle illuminated her entire foyer, including the staircase where two black cats with yellow eyes sat watching her. When the light hit them they both stood up and trotted down the stairs, meowing at her loudly.

"Hazel! Sabrina!" Eve exclaimed, dropping to her knees so she could wrap them in her arms. "Where did you come from? I thought you were lost!" Both cats purred loudly and let her caress them even though she was still wet and they normally shied from all forms of water.

"I found them. Well, actually, they found me," Atticus said.

"Where were they?" Eve buried her face in their soft, black fur.

"They ran in front of my car," Atticus explained. "I was coming back from the movie and two black cats shot out in front of me and I thought, what bad luck! And then I thought wait a minute, those cats look familiar."

Eve cringed a little when he mentioned the movie, the same movie she'd refused to go to with him. Atticus continued without pause.

"I stopped the car and when I got out to look for them they ran right to me. I figured you'd be looking for them so I brought them here. Your door was wide open and the power had gone off. I put the cats in the house and then noticed your purse was sitting right there and..." here he kind of shuffled his feet, "I got a little worried. So I thought I'd wait a bit on your porch just to see if you made it home safely."

Good Lord, she thought, *he is an angel.*

Overcome at his story and the return of the sister cats, Eve stood up and hugged him, crying and sniffling as she did.

"Thank you, thank you so much," she mumbled into his shoulder. He only hesitated a moment before wrapping his long arms around her and holding her tight. She relaxed into his strong embrace. He was so warm.

"You're shivering," he said softly.

"I know."

Atticus pulled out of her arms. He lifted the candle that he still held with one hand closer to her face and looked her over carefully. "Are you sure you're all right? Did anything happen to you?"

"No," she said, sniffling a little. "I just got caught in the rain and I was so worried about Hazel and Sabrina." Her lip trembled when she spoke.

"Here," Atticus handed her the candle. "Go change into something dry. I'll make you some tea. Everything's fine now."

The sister cats followed her upstairs and laid on her bed as she changed by candlelight. She put on black fleece pants, heavy socks, a white long sleeve cotton shirt and her burnt orange sweater. When she took the candle into the bathroom to brush out and pull up her hair, she was shocked at her reflection.

All of the crying and walking in the rain had made her eye makeup run in black streaks down her face and blend with the green face makeup making a muddy swirl of strange colors. In all of the distress of the evening, she'd completely forgotten she had green makeup on at all. She looked like she'd fallen into a mud puddle face first or had tried to go undercover with the navy seals and come to a tragic end. No wonder Atticus had been so shocked at her appearance.

Eve scrubbed the makeup off with soap and warm water then brushed her damp hair and pulled it back into a loose ponytail at the nape of her neck. She studied her appearance and decided she didn't look great, but she definitely looked better.

Meanwhile, Atticus had apparently located all of the candles in the house. As Eve descended the stairs with her candle in hand and the cats right on her heels, she gasped in delight at the scene in her living room. Several candles on the coffee table, mantle, side tables and shelves were lit, their light dancing off of the glass knick knacks and the large beveled mirror over the fireplace. The tall candles she kept in the fireplace were also lit, making it feel cozy and romantic.

"Hot tea," Atticus announced coming from the kitchen. He carried two mugs of steaming tea and gave her one once she was settled onto the couch. He placed his mug on the coffee table and took the throw from the back of the couch, covering Eve with it before he sat down next to her.

"Thank you," Eve said. "This is beautiful."

"You're even more beautiful in candlelight." His eyes twinkled at her. "So, it's entirely my pleasure."

Eve blushed at the compliment, but couldn't help smiling. She spotted a smear of glittery green on his shoulder and reached out to touch it, dismayed. "I got makeup on your shirt."

Atticus dipped his chin down and to the side to try to see the spot, telling her, "Don't worry about it."

"I'm sorry," Eve said. She let her hand slide from his shoulder down his arm and finally to rest on top of his hand. "I'm also sorry I didn't go on a Halloween date with you."

His eyes, those piercing blue eyes, locked onto hers. She

had stopped shivering from cold when she put on dry clothes, but now, she felt that delicious tingle along her shoulders and neck. The candlelight deepened the richness of his red hair and beard, making her want to reach out and touch it with her fingers. She ran her eyes along his nose to the corner of his firm mouth where his mustache curled just a little.

"That's okay," Atticus said, his voice low and soft. "This is better than what I had planned for us."

Us. What a simple little word. Yet the sound of it filled her heart with joy. She lifted her hand and let her fingers touch his temple and push up into his fiery red hair.

"Us?" She asked sweetly.

"If you want there to be," he answered, leaning towards her, pulled into her by the feel of her fingers in his hair. "Do you?"

"Yes, I want there to be an us," she said as his lips touched hers.

That was it, what he'd been waiting for, and with this encouragement, Atticus kissed her. He was so gentle as they pressed their lips together for the very first time, savoring the first taste. Then, as the moments passed, his mouth was firmer, more insistent, and he reached around her waist, pulling her closer. Eve pushed her fingers into his hair and around the back of his neck, sensually massaging the muscles down his neck and along his shoulders. She opened her mouth ever so slightly and he touched his tongue to hers, tasting her, wanting more, but holding himself in check.

She had never felt so safe and so wanted. His whole body was reacting to her, rippling with desire, tuned in to her and only her, she could feel it, sense it in the air. Yet he had such a gentle touch, kissed her so tenderly, respect and longing wrapped into one. The effect was dizzying.

Atticus pulled her into the crook of his arm and she rested her head there where she could hear his heart beating fast in his chest. They didn't speak for a while, just cuddled, his fingers played with the ends of her hair sending more tingles along her neck and shoulders.

"This is so nice," she said, almost whispered.

"Mm-hmm," he answered, the sound rumbling through his chest.

The rain still drummed on the roof and spattered against the windows. The wind blew wildly outside, but the door remained closed and the sister cats lay together in the armchair nearby, sleeping quietly. Peace and contentment surrounded them and in that moment she had a thought.

"You know what?" Eve lifted her head and looked at Atticus in the eye.

"What?"

"I think the house likes you."

"Does it?" He smiled.

"Yes." Eve looked around at the calm living room. Nothing had fallen, no candles had blown out, everything had stayed in its place.

"Does the house actually have an opinion?" He asked, still smiling.

"I didn't used to think it did, but over the past few days I may have changed my mind. Maybe my Dad was right, maybe this house is haunted," she answered.

Atticus looked around the room, considering this comment before answering. Then he said, "It's too beautiful to be haunted. This is a lovely home. Maybe instead of haunted we should say it's enchanted."

Another shiver went down Eve's spine, then back up again. Goosebumps covered her arms. He was right. She knew he was right. Everything about Atticus Murphy was right.

"Enchanted...I like that," she answered.

"Good," he said, and kissed her again.

***

Thank you for reading Enchanting Eve! If you enjoyed this book you may enjoy the other books in the series...

Love is at the Table - Thanksgiving Romance

Mistletoe Madness - Christmas Romance

New Year in Paradise - New Year's Eve Romance

***

Or you may enjoy Darci's Dream Come True series. The first book, Her Scottish Keep , is a fun and flirty romance set in the Scottish Highlands...a clean and whole-some contemporary Scottish love story :)

Epilogue

"Eve, honey, did you get the popcorn?" Atticus called to her from the kitchen just as Eve placed the giant bowl of hot, salted popcorn on the coffee table.

"Yes," she answered. "The hot chocolate is still on the counter." She stood up in time to see Atticus walking through the hallway, not carrying two mugs of hot chocolate, but instead holding a tiny orange ball of fur. She smiled, the man hadn't put their new kitten down for more than two minutes since they picked him up yesterday at the animal shelter.

"Merlin," Atticus spoke to the orange fluff sticking out of his cupped hands. "These are your grandparents." Atticus stopped in front of Eve's parent's wedding photo and held the tiny kitten up to see.

"Merlin isn't old enough to understand about grandparents," Eve pretended to scold her boyfriend—correction, fiancé—as she gingerly took the beautiful little kitty from him. Merlin mewed in protest, his blue eyes blinked and he stuck his big ears high into the air as if to say he was, indeed, interested in grandparents. "Now go get the hot chocolate, please," Eve said.

"Of course!" Atticus leaned over and kissed her before turning towards the kitchen. Merlin mewed again.

"Not in front of the children, darling," Eve teased, then held Merlin's tiny body carefully to her chest as she carried him into the living room. The sister cats perked up and took notice when she sat down with him on the couch. They didn't go so far as to get up from their comfortable spot on the fat armchair, but they knew Merlin was a new member of the family. They would deign to play with him when he was a little older.

"When will the trick-or-treaters get here?" Atticus asked as he carried in the hot chocolate. He was almost as excited as a child was about trick-or-treating. "Is the candy out?"

"Yes," Eve said calmly. "I got it ready earlier just in case." She looked out the living room window to the grey light of dusk. "I think they will be coming any time, the little ones at least."

"Those are my favorite," Atticus declared as he took some popcorn and popped it into his mouth, chewing happily.

He had been over the top elated for the past few days, she had too. She looked into her hands where she held their new pink nosed, blue eyed orange tabby cat, and was surprised once again at the diamond engagement ring that now graced her left ring finger. They had been engaged for just over three days and she wasn't quite used to seeing the beautiful ring on her hand yet.

He'd proposed in the middle of the Fischer pumpkin patch because that's where he said he had fallen head over heels for her. The kids from the classroom had assisted him with the surprise proposal while they were on the annual pumpkin picking field trip. They had secretly brought rolled up poster boards in their jackets with colorful letters drawn on them spelling out 'MARRY ME EVE' and held them up in line behind Atticus as he got on one knee and asked her to be his wife.

It had been perfect. The proposal fit exactly who he was, who they were together. She'd cried and said 'yes' and then the Fischer's had brought out refreshments of cookies and hot apple cider. It filled her heart to know that this was the first of many celebrations yet to come with this man, her Atticus.

Their first official act as a newly engaged couple had been to answer an ad by the animal shelter pleading with the public to help them find homes for a number of abandoned kittens. When Eve spied the orange fur and blue eyes of this little guy peeking out from the sea of grey and black kittens, she'd known immediately that he was supposed to be theirs. He looked just like Atticus! And when she picked him up and showed him to Atticus, the man was completely smitten.

Atticus loved cats. He also loved tradition and family and children and Eve thought she was probably the luckiest girl in the world to have him as her future husband. Another thing he loved, she had found out, was decorating for holidays. Determined to help her change her house's reputation as being haunted, Atticus spent hundreds of dollars and they had both dedicated several hours to decorating the house and yard. There were countless strings of purple and orange lights, funny scarecrows, jack-o-lanterns with wide, happy smiles and cartoon witches and ghosts all over the house. Nothing too scary. Everything fun.

The doorbell rang and Atticus jumped up from the couch. "I'll get it!"

Eve heard a chorus of little voices shouting "Trick or treat!" Then Atticus exclaiming appreciatively over their costumes as he passed out candy bars. Apparently all of their efforts had worked. The little kids were definitely not afraid to approach the house this Halloween.

Eve sighed pleasantly, looking around at the warm, cozy living room. So much joy had been in this room for so many years. All of the holidays and plain old evenings she'd spent here with her father flashed through her heart. And now there was new joy and a new life laid out in front of her, one that was more full than she'd ever imagined it could be. She wished her Dad was here, and her Mom. They would have liked Atticus, she was certain.

The sister cats gazed at her thoughtfully with their large, yellow eyes and Eve swore they looked like they were giving her knowing smiles. Merlin mewed and stretched his neck high in the air, bobbing his little head back and forth, trying to look her in the eye. She leaned her face down and touched her nose to his. He mewed at her again. Eve smiled.

"You're right, Merlin," she said to him, "and ladies," to the sister cats, "I do believe you are correct. Mom and Dad are here with us now. Beautiful memories are what make this house enchanted and we will all be very happy here together for a long, long time."

The End

Also by Darci Balogh

Dream Come True Series

1. Her Scottish Keep

2. Her British Bard

Lady Billionaire Series

1. Ms. Money Bags

2. Ms. Perfect

Sweet Holiday Romance Series (Box Set - great value!)

Want a quick escape over the holidays? These feel-good romances will get you in the spirit for Halloween, Thanksgiving, Christmas and a brand New Year!

1. Enchanting Eve (you've got it!)

2. Love is at the Table

3. Mistletoe Madness

4. New Year in Paradise

Sugar Plum Romance Series

Christmas, cooking, and chefs falling in love!

1. Charlotte's Christmas Charade

2. Bella's Christmas Blunder

Love & Marriage Contemporary Romance (Box Set - best bang for your buck!)

Steamy, emotional, relatable characters, these older woman, younger man romances are both racy and romantic.

1. The Quiet of Spring

About the Author

Darci Balogh is a writer and indie filmmaker from Denver. She grew up in the beautiful mountains of Colorado and has lived in several areas of the state over her lifetime. She currently resides in Denver where she raised her two glorious, intelligent daughters to functioning adulthood. This is, by far, one of her highest achievements. She has a love-hate relationship with gardening, probably should dust more, adores dogs and is allergic to cats.

Darci has been a writer since she was a child and enjoys crafting stories into novels and screenplays. Big surprise, some of her favorite pastimes are reading and watching movies. Classic British TV is high on her 'Like' list, along with quietly depressing detective series and coffee with heavy cream.